MW01199471

Jesse D'Angelo

Encyclopocalypse Publications
www.encyclopocalypse.com

SPECIAL THANKS

Sean Duregger
Crystal Cook
Shannon Marie Ettaro
Leah Dawn Baker
Daniel Sanchez
Sherri Sellers McCune
My brother, Kevin
And my lovely wife, Lauren
For putting up with me
You rock

SPECIAL THANKS

DYING SHEEP 2

CHAPTER 1

OKAY, first things first, that bitch Samantha has to die.

Just the fact that she's still out there, walking around, breathing free air, *not* in excruciating pain, the fact that I failed... I'm not having it. Marvin Brumlow doesn't fail, not at killing, anyway. I am seven feet of hateful, disfigured, redneck violence. Dirty and sweaty, stinking and cruel, that's me. I'm a psychopath and a sadist, and I'm the newest superstar in Hell, killing in the Boogeyman Championships to the delight of legions of fans. I'm literally immortal now. And yet, some dingbat, squeaky little goodie-two-shoes manages to survive?

No sir, that will not do.

Getting an unsanctioned pass through the veil is not hard if you know the right people, though it is expensive. But I'm a superstar, so I can afford it. It's been a little over a month since my first clash where Samantha got away, a year in Earth-time. I guess it's now 1981 up there already. So weird. In any case, Jim has my next clash set up for this coming Friday night, so I'm taking care of this dang thorn in my side first. I'll step through the veil, kill that little bitch, and come back without anybody even knowing. Unsanctioned travel between worlds is highly illegal, but what are they gonna do, send me to Hell?

I sit on the couch in my luxury apartment. The floors are polished marble. The bathroom has heated floors and a jumbo jacuzzi. The bedroom is outfitted with two king-size beds pushed together to accommodate my big ass, and I have a personal bar stocked with the finest spirits and crystal glasses. I'm wearing a red silk robe and pajamas and I sip aged brandy through a straw. Hey, after blowing the lower half of my face off years ago in a botched suicide attempt, it's pretty much impossible to drink anything without a straw. Floor-to-ceiling windows give me a panoramic view of downtown Malavista.

I watch the traffic, the flashing billboards, the greed, the road rage. I smell the gasoline and rubber, sweet and salty delicacies from the street vendors, the filth and rot of the alleyways. I see crime and poverty and homeless-ness, and it all looks the same here as it does back on Earth. The rich fat cats still drive by in their sports cars and pay no mind. The whores still flick their cigarette butts into alleyway puddles before getting into cars with the rich fat cats and taking slop-shots to the face. I love it.

Slurping the rest of my brandy through the straw, I look at the clock on the wall. 10:35 p.m. One more thing Hell and Earth have in common: dealers are always late. I grumble and stand up, pacing around. Waiting is one of my least favorite things to do, but this is important. I pace, swing my arms, check the clock again. What the fuck? Jim told me this guy was reliable and discreet. I swear, if he fucking flakes... *Knock knock knock!*

Aha, here we go. I open the door and there's this

skinny little tweaker dude in the hallway. His eyes go wide when he sees me. He's got a raggedy mohawk, shabby clothes, backpack, and a skateboard. Yup, dealers are the same everywhere.

"Wow... I mean hi, uh, Mr. Brumlow," the kid says.

Jim says the little troll goes by the name Snapdragon, but I'm not even gonna try to enunciate that with my mangled mouth, so I quietly step aside and let him in. He seems nervous, so he's either terrified of me, or a big fan, or both. Either way, I want to get this over with. I hand him the money agreed upon, and he pulls out this weird little thing from his pocket. Looks like a fancy garage door opener or something. The kid explains to me that this is called a "cell phone," and it has a special "app" in it which allows interdimensional travel. I don't know what any of that means, but I take his word for it.

One of things I've learned during my time in Hell is that the availability of technology is decades ahead of what's on Earth. Sort of like how it takes forty-fifty years for technology and fashion from America to make its way to third world countries, the same is true here. The most cutting-edge stuff is available here first, then a few decades later, in America and other first-world countries, then a few decades after that, maybe it trickles down to the little brown people in the third-world. So now I have to learn what all this new shit is. Same thing with those little hummingbird-camera-fuckers that follow me around during clashes.

Snapdragon instructs me on how to use this "app" thing, explaining that once I step through the veil and arrive at the desired coordinates on Earth, I have only one hour before the signal would cut out, and the veil would close for good. Any longer than that costs a *lot* more. That's fine. An hour is all I need.

That's an hour in Hell-time, not Earth-time. An hour in Hell is several hours on Earth. So a three-hour clash actually takes about a day on Earth for the victims. Don't ask me to explain the specifics, I don't fucking know. Anyway, once I get back to Hell, I have to immediately take the memory card out of the phone and discard them both, before my little transgression is tracked by the authorities.

"You need anything else?" Snapdragon asks. "Guns? Coke? Speed? Girls? Cheese? You name it, man, I can get it."

I shake my head no.

"Well, uh... you got the number if you ever need anything. Say, uh... my little nephew is a big fan," he says, pulling out a small pad of paper and a pen. "Could I maybe get your autograph for him if it's not—"

I give him a hard look.

He clears his throat and takes the hint.

"Right, no worries," he says, deflating as he backs out the front door. "Uh, so if you ever need anything else, just... yeah."

I close the door in his face.

ONE STEP through the veil and I'm in suburbia. Chilmark, MA. Little coastal fishing town. It's dark. I can smell the sea. According to Snapdragon, the coordinates he entered will bring me within fifty yards of my target. Perfect. I look around to take in the scene.

Looks like I'm standing in an alley behind a row of townhouses overlooking the harbor. I look down and find my big bare feet in a puddle. It must have just rained, because all the streets are wet. For an alley, it's pretty clean back here. Trash cans stand upright, not over-flowing with garbage. No rats or cockroaches scuttling around. No needles, no used condoms, no whores swal-lowing prick-snot for a few bucks behind a dumpster.

Nope, this is a rich neighborhood, everything nice and clean. Fucking yuppies. I hate them all. Makes me want to kill this bitch even more.

I need to work fast. Suburbia has never been my element; I stick out like a sore thumb. Well, like even more of a sore thumb than everywhere else. Too many people, too many lights, not enough places to hide. But it's late and quiet and it looks like all the little yuppies are tucked snug in their beds. All but one. There's a light on in one of the townhouses, second floor. Could that be you, my sweet little darling?

There is a fire escape, so I put that shit to use. I creep up the wet, rusty stairs, and the structure creaks under my weight. I try to go slower, to step more gingerly, but let's face it, I weigh four hundred fucking pounds. Reaching the second story window, I see the curtain is conveniently pulled aside. Thank you very much.

I'm at the kitchen window, looking in on a sink full of dirty dishes. Past that is a living room with clothes strewn everywhere. Hm, piggy-piggy, not what I expected, Sam. There's posters on the walls of actors and pop stars, and some wussy named Phil Collins is on the TV singing about how he can feel something in the air tonight? Oh yeah, I feel something in the air tonight too. Murder.

There she is. Samantha. Wearing sweats and an over-sized football jersey, she comes around the corner with a phone in her hand, twirling the cord around her finger. She paces in and out of view, rolling her eyes, obviously getting an earful from whoever she's talking to. Then she starts speaking and it makes sense.

"I know, mom," she says, "but I just need some time to myself, okay? You did say I could stay here for a while, right? ...Well, I don't know how long."

The conversation continues and I'm getting bored. Time's running out. I could just smash through the window, charge at her... Nah. That's no fun. Patience, Marv. I keep watching, and things begin to heat up. Samantha tosses a purple bath robe over the couch and begins pulling off her sweats. Yes!

"Look, mom, I'm trying to put my life back together, and this is the only way I know how to do it. I'm sorry. No, I know. Yes, of course, I love you too..." She finally says her goodbyes and cradles the phone. Bye bye, mommy. Last time you're ever gonna hear your little girl's voice.

I watch on as she tosses her sweatpants aside, then her socks. Then she pulls off her jersey, and whoah! Two of the biggest flapjack titties I've ever seen in my life flop down and slap against her hips. Damn, I knew she had big titties, but had no idea they'd be so saggy. Guess she was wearing a bra last time I saw her, knows how to hide it pretty well. She's a pretty little thing, not an old maid. Doesn't want the boys to know she got utters hanging down to her knees. I lean in for a closer look and accidentally bump into the windowsill.

Samantha hears it and instantly bolts upright, clutching her bathrobe. I quickly move away, hugging against the building where she can't see me. A minute passes, then I glance over at the window. Her shadow moves across the glass. Can't see her from this angle, but judging from the shadow, she has something in her hand. A knife? Good girl. Let's make it interesting.

The shadow moves in closer, and finally I see just the tip of her nose coming right up to the pane, her breath steaming it up. A long, tense moment passes. She's shaking, terrified. Good. A year after a run-in with me and she's still all fucked up in the head. Makes me feel a little better.

I see her nose pull back inside, then her shadow. I can only assume she's shaking her head as she walks off, mumbling to herself that she's hearing things. Nope, it really is me again, bitch. I come back to the window and look, and she's gone, but now I see the bathroom door open a crack, and steam is rising. Ahhh yes, take a shower, little Sammie.

I pull out my phone/interdimensional transport-doohickey-thingie, whatever the hell it is, and look at the screen. A half hour is already up. Shit, I need to get this show on the road. But here's the part where I actually like this technology shit. For the next half hour, I can come and go through the veil as much as I like. Once I'm behind the veil, solid objects like walls and other things on Earth, they're just like shadows. I can walk right through them.

So I press the little button to open the veil, and there it is. I step in, and now I'm in the shadow world. I'm a spirit, a ghost. And what do ghosts do? They walk through walls. With a smile on my mangled face, I step forward, passing through the wall like it's nothing, and find myself inside the apartment. I am standing in the sink, though, so I take another step forward to get clear. Then I step back through the veil.

Now I'm *really* inside. Not a ghost anymore, flesh and blood, baby. I look at her kitchen counter, admiring the options laying before me for murder weapons. Big knife, another big knife, spatula—that would be interesting—apple peeler, can opener, cork screw. I keep looking, hearing the sounds of running water coming from the other room. Opening drawers, I find the silverware, and begin to browse. Forks and knives, a rolling pin, an *ice pick!* I scoop that bad boy up. Yeaaah, I haven't done it with one of these for quite a while.

It's time. Naked girl in the shower. Ice pick in hand.

I start across the kitchen, the floorboards creaking under me. For a second, I worry that she'll hear me, but so what? I'm going to kill her anyway. Still, I want it to be on my terms, so I push forward. All over the kitchen counters and couches are sketch pads and papers, with a bunch of pencils and paints and shit. Looks like little Samantha is a bit of an artist... I hate artists.

I pick up one of her doodles and look at it. Looks like a face drawn in charcoal, some kind of messy pastel colors in there... I think they would call this shit "abstract" art.

Or it is "impressionist?" Who cares. I crumple it up and toss it away. Closer. Down the hallway, I move. Closer.

I feel the steam, hear the sound of the hot water hissing. Samantha is humming some little tune in there. Closer. I step on a particularly creaky floorboard and wince. A second later, I hear the water abruptly turn off.

"Hello?" I hear Samantha say.

Shit. She's coming this way, I have to hide. Have to do this right. Behind me is a small linen closet, and just past that, the hall turns to the left. I back up as quiet as I can and turn around the corner, waiting. A minute later, the bathroom door squeaks open and a very timid little girl begins inching out into the hall.

"H-Hello? I-Is someone there?"

Oh, she's so scared, this is perfect. Okay, this is it. This is it. Whew! I squeeze the ice pick, tense my muscles. Man, I can't wait to see the look on her face when she sees *me*. She takes another step, then another. I can see her shadow creeping along the floor. Closer. She's almost here. Her shadow slides across the door of the closet. I raise the ice pick, ready to strike.

Rrreeeoowww!!!

Apparently, Samatha has a fucking cat, because the little bastard springs out of the closet like a fucking, I don't know, *spring,* and runs away. Now, look. I'm Marvin Brumlow, okay? Nothing scares me. I've murdered hundreds of people, literally been to Hell and back. I don't get frightened. So this cat doesn't *scare* me, but well... I do scream like a little girl. It *startles* me, okay? It's a reflex, completely takes me off guard. Fuck off.

I drop the ice pick. It bounces on the floor. I look up

and see Samantha staring straight at me, shock and fear in her eyes. Well shit, this is awkward. I shrug and smile.

"Hewwo, Tsamantha."

Annnd she snaps.

White-hot horror pops out of her eyes and she screams so loud and high-pitch, it actually hurts my ears. She runs for the bathroom, her robe flapping open, her big mamajamas flapping around. I'm on her in a second, my head smashing through the top of the door frame as we topple into the sink.

She flails wildly and screams, cries, begs. I love it.

"Dib you missth me?" I ask with a chuckle, wrapping my tree trunk-arms around her and groping at that smooth, wet skin. Look at those melons swishing around! I dropped the ice pick, so I look for something else. Soap. Shampoo. Not a whole lot of good murder weapons in a bathroom... Hmm, I could cave her head in with the toilet lid? Or smash the mirror and use the shards of glass to cut her up? Damn, it's hard to decide. I'm distracted by these huge, flailing titties...

That's it! Her titties!

I reach around her and grab at those flappy fuckers. With my right hand, I get a good grip on that left titty. With my left hand, I grab the right titty. Then all I have to do is pull up and back, and presto! I stretch those fuckers around her head and cinch 'em good and tight. Samantha's face goes red, then purple.

Ligaments tear and blood vessels explode as I stretch the skin way past its limit. She pisses herself, and of course it gets all over my feet. Damn it. I squeeze tighter, applying more pressure. You're mine now, bitch.

Samantha kicks and fights and spasms, but I can tell by the look in her eyes as they swell out of her head, that she knows this is it. Finally, a swollen, purple tongue flops out of her mouth and her eyes bug out. I see her light go out.

I hold the squeeze another minute, just to make sure.

Then I let her go. Her body collapses to the floor with a loud thud. I stand admiring my work. Choked to death with her own titties. Man, if only the fans at the arena back home could see this one.

I hear banging at the door and some landlord is out there asking what's going on, saying he's calling the cops, blah blah blah. Time to get out of here anyway.

Satisfied, I pull out my little gizmo, open up the thing, do the other thing, and go back to Hell. Finished the mission with three minutes to spare.

Now I'm supposed to remove the memory card somehow, find a place to discard the phone...? Fuck it. I just crush the damn thing in my hand and launch it as hard as I can out the window.

Well, then. That went pretty well.

Think I'll jerk off and go to bed.

CHAPTER 2

"WELL, ARE YOU EXCITED?" Mr. Black asks.

Jim and I are sitting across from the president of the Boogeyman Championships, David Black himself, in his plush office, overlooking downtown Malavista. The big boss man leans back in his chair, feet up on the desk, tossing a rubber stress-ball up and down. He's wearing jeans and sneakers and a simple shirt. No shiny suits or expensive shoes today; guess he likes to keep it casual at the office. Still, his bald head is newly-polished and his diamond earrings, glitzy watch, and gaudy rings are ever-present. He grins, waiting for my response.

I look over at Jim to answer for me.

"Hell yeah, man," Jim says, chewing a fresh wad of gum. "We are ready to *rock!*"

If it wasn't for the fact that Jim is useful to me—and the fact that if I hurt him, I hurt myself—I would've ripped his fucking head off a long time ago. His snarky smile, his dipshit, hippy clothes, the way every word he speaks sounds like he's trying to sell a used car, his nonchalant attitude, the way he chews his gum... Ugh. Still, after blowing off the bottom half of my face with a .38 and having what was left of my jaw surgically stitched into a bizarre piece of impressionist sculpture, people tend to have a hard time understanding me when I speak. So, I have Jim.

"Good! I'm excited too!" Mr. Black says. "Your first clash did some of the best numbers we've ever seen in the BMC. You're quickly becoming a crowd favorite. There is a lot of buzz about your next clash on Friday. Everybody wants to see you back in action. You could very well overthrow Snapper and be our next champion! Are you ready?"

On the one hand, of course I want to win the championship. That's the big money, baby. On the other hand, it's all bullshit. This isn't a "sport" where you score points and have rules like football, it's just a gore show. The person holding the belt is simply whoever draws the biggest ratings and is the most popular with the fans. So naturally, I'm going to kick Snapper's ass and be the champ very soon.

I nod. Damn right I'm ready.

"Good," Mr. Black says, pulling out a file folder and tossing it onto his desk. "Here's the dossier on your new targets. You're gonna like this one."

"Why? Does he have to kill a bunch of nuns, or something?" Jim asks, scooping up the folder and opening it up.

"Nah nah, just a bunch of idiot kids, as usual," Mr. Black says with a sly smile. "But look where the clash will be taking place."

Jim reads a little, then looks up. "Chapman Institute for the criminally insane?"

I stiffen up a little as I hear the name.

"Sound familiar, Marvin?" Mr. Black asks.

I nod again. "Thatsh where I wasth when I..." I trail off. I don't like talking about this. As rotten and foul as I am, I'm still not proud of the fact that I murdered my wife and two children, tried to kill myself, and ended up at the Chapman Institute. I stare through the huge wall of windows overlooking the city, my mind wandering back to that awful day.

"That's riiiiiight," the BMC president says, his eyes lighting up. "After they let you out, the public went berserk with outrage. Somebody tried to burn the place to the ground, it was closed down and condemned, blah blah blah. So now it's just ruins, sitting in the countryside of the Chicago suburbs."

"I don't get it," Jim says.

"It's become a local legend. The place that used to hold the infamous Marvin Brumlow. It's the place that almost burned to the ground, and dozens of patients died in the fire. It's also where the local college kids like to go and party."

"Ahhh, I see," Jim says and resumes smacking away at his gum.

"This Friday night," Mr. Black says, pointing at the folder, "that particular group of dumbass kids is planning to get together and explore the creepy ruins with their flashlights. Drink some beer, do some drugs, roast marsh-mellows, get laid..."

"Get murdered," Jim finishes.

"Right. Good, wholesome family entertainment. What do you think, Marvin?"

They both look at me. I shift in my chair and squeeze

the armrests with sweaty palms. Going back to that fucking place is not something I ever wanted to do. Still, getting to see it in ruins and slaughtering a bunch of people there does sound like a nice homecoming. So, fuck it.

I shrug and say, "Thure."

"Huh?" Mr. Black sits forward, not understanding me.

"He says sure, Mr. Black," Jim clarifies.

"Ah, good," the boss man says, sitting back in his chair and tossing his rubber ball up and down some more. "And I assume the purse we agreed upon is still acceptable? Five percent bump up from the last clash?"

"Well, actually..." Jim begins, smacking his gum.

"Yesth," I say, cutting him off. Don't need him negotiating for me. The money is fine. Greedy little fucking troll.

Jim clears his throat and shrugs. "Yup, we're good."

"Good," Mr. Black says, standing up. "Then there is just one last order of business. I have a surprise for you, Marvin. It'd be nice to not be walking around barefoot, right?"

I look down at my big, hairy feet and wiggle my toes. Honestly, I'm used to it. Never tried on a pair of shoes that actually fit me right.

Mr. Black presses an intercom button on his desk and speaks into it excitedly, "Okay, send him in." He looks at me with a smile. "You're gonna love this."

The door opens and the cute secretary escorts in a weird little dude carrying a box nearly as big as himself. He's maybe five feet tall, with silver hair greased and styled to perfection, and the cleanest little pencil-thin mustache I've ever seen. His shirt is some kind of pink satin or some shit. His nails are manicured, his white slacks neatly pressed, his shoes made from expensive leather and curling up at the toes. He has a confident, smug look on his face as he approaches.

"Henri!" Mr. Black says, pronouncing the name with a silent *H* and opening his arms wide to give the little guy a hug. "Marvin, I'd like to introduce you to the one and only Henri Pantoufflé. The finest shoemaker in Hell. We flew him in from Beaumont Douleur just to give you this surprise."

Jim and I both stand politely. I'm nervous. I did ask for a pair of shoes, but I was mostly joking. Didn't expect them to do it.

"Hello, Monsieur Brumlow," the little guy says in a thick French accent. "It is a pleasure for to meet you."

"Uh, hi..." I say.

"Monsieur Black say you have very big foot. Hard to find shoe, oui?"

I nod tentatively.

"Well," he continues, "I make for you new pair of shoe, custom make just for you. I use the best leather, double-stitch seam, padded insole, steel toe. Big strong boot for big strong man, oui?"

Hm, that sounds pretty good. Could it really be true?

"Please, please," the little weirdo gestures for me to sit down.

Hell, why not? I'm actually starting to get a little excited. A pair of boots my size, custom made just for me? Oh man, it's been years since I had a pair of shoes that fit comfortably. I sit down, trying not to look too giddy. The French shoemaker kneels down in front of me, while Jim and Mr. Black lean in to see as well.

With great glee, Frenchie holds up the box and reaches for the lid, drawing it out, teasing me before the big reveal. He cracks it open slowly, slowly, then finally pulls the lid back all the way. What I see in front of me are the biggest, blackest, shiniest, chrome-studded-est biker boots that an S&M dominatrix could possibly ask for.

"Whoa!" Jim excitedly slaps my shoulder. "Check those out, dude!"

"Very nice!" Mr. Black adds. "What do you think, Marvin?"

Frenchie is looking right at me, beaming that way-too-white smile of his.

"Uh, umm..." I grumble, trying to wrap my head around what I'm seeing. I pull one of the boots out to look closer. Polished black leather, chrome studs all over, chrome on the toe, chrome on the heel... I don't know what to say, but my blood begins to boil. On the side, there's even a custom-embroidered logo that reads "Big Bad Marvin" in red. I struggle for the right words.

"You like?" the shoe designer asks. "Black leather, big and strong. Very macho, oui? Boot for big, strong man!"

"Marvin, what's wrong?" Mr. Black says.

"It'sth justh...I don' know..."

"Big boot for big man," the little guy persists enthusiastically, putting on a mock-tough guy face and flexing as if he has muscles. "Very strong, very macho. You like the Rock and Roll, oui? Judas Priest, *Hell bent for leather*! Rob Halford. Very manly-man. Strong, macho! Oui?"

"Come on, man. Try 'em on," Jim says and smacks his gum.

Mr. Black and Monsieur Whatever egg me on, so I sigh and give in. I take the other shoe out of the box, open it up and slide my foot in. Surprisingly, it goes in with no problem. Wow, looks like they actually got the size right!

Then I lace it up and it just don't feel right, but whatever, I'm halfway there, so I might as well finish. I put on the other boot and tie the laces. Doesn't feel right. I stand up and begin to walk around.

"There you go!" Mr. Black says.

"Cool, dude! Those look great!" Jim adds.

"C'est magnifique!" Frenchy says, clapping his hands like a girl.

"Well? What do you think?" Mr. Black asks.

I pace around for another minute, leaning and turning, flexing my feet, but there's no point. The boots are long enough, but too narrow. They squeeze the insides of my arches, and something keeps scratching my heels each time I take a step. Not comfortable. Plus, they're a glossy, chromey, macho-black eyesore. And so, a very familiar feeling begins to come over me. My pulse speeds up. I start to feel angry.

"Buddy?" Jim asks, starting to worry.

I look over at the fruity little fashion victim in front of me and my eyes fill up with rage and hatred. I lift up my right foot and pull the boot off.

"M-Marvin?" Mr. Black is also starting to worry.

I toss the boot away and start on the other one.

"Eh, Monsieur Brumlow, is there problem?" the little guy begins to tremble and takes a step back. "If is no good, I can make alteration..."

I yank the second ugly fucker off my foot. I walk forward with the boot in hand, my eyes locked onto my target. Frenchy backs up, the color draining from his face.

"M-Monsieur, please..." he holds up his hands, begging.

"Marvin, if you don't like them, Henri can just..."

I don't care what Mr. Black has to say. You can't just stop a train once it starts rolling. So I reach out to grab my new little friend, and he naturally screams and tries to run. But no, I catch him easily by the back of the neck and lift him up into the air. He screams and flails, but it's no use. I've heard tough guys say they're gonna put a boot up someone's ass before, but nobody ever really does that. So here's my chance.

"Marvin, no!"

I angle the chrome-steel toe forward and ram it straight up into his puckered, French pooper. I hear pants and underwear rip as I jam that fucker good and deep in there, ripping his butt hole wide open while he yelps like a little bitch. He squirms and squeals as I casually walk him over to the wall of windows, the boot stuck heel-deep in his ass.

I look out at the sprawling metropolis in front of me and smile at the thought of people jumping out of the way and screaming as this cheeky fucker splatters down onto the sidewalk. I'll just hurl him through the window unceremoniously. No clever catch phrase, just toss him out like a bag of garbage and go home. So I pull my arm back, ready to launch my little friend through the glass —

"Marvin, stop!" Mr. Black shouts.

— I launch anyway.

Crunch!

Apparently, David Black installed double-reinforced security windows in here. Instead of crashing through the glass and falling to his death, Monsiuer Frenchy crumples like a bug smacking into a windshield. Millions of little cracks run through the pane of safety glass, but it does not break. Instead, every bone in Frenchy's body breaks, organs rupture, and he slides to the floor, a bloody mess. Hm. Alrighty then, that'll do.

Jim stands silent. Mr. Black has his face in his hands. Guess he imagined his surprise gift going a little different. So, with my big, ugly, bare feet, I stroll over to the desk, scoop up the file folder with the dossier of my next victims, and head for the door.

"Thsee you on Fwiday."

CHAPTER 3

IT'S the night before the clash.

I lay on my couch, reviewing the dossier of my next victims one more time. The T.V. is on in the background, re-runs of *Hogan's Heroes* or some shit, but I'm not paying attention. I'm in my happy place. The fire is going, the lights are dim, I'm wearing my favorite robe, I have my brandy, a salad bowl full of double-chocolate ice cream... and my list of sweet, sweet victims.

There are eight in total this time, a group of friends from DePaul University, and man, it's like looking at the menu of a four-star restaurant. Everything looks delicious.

First up is Johnny. Former high school linebacker, now a theater major, chiseled jaw, fluffy blonde hair... Yup, I hate him. Nothing worse than some arrogant, pretty-boy actor. I look through his photos and it's like a swimwear catalogue, with stud-muffin Johnny taking every chance he can get to flex and show off those abs and guns. He does look like a fairly big, strong dude—I mean, for a normal person—and he might put up a decent fight. Good. Nothing demoralizes a bunch of victims more than seeing the strongest of them getting rag-dolled and smashed like a bug.

Then there's Johnny's girlfriend, Natasha. Or is she really his girlfriend? I don't know, the description in the dossier is pretty vague. In any case, seems she's a feminist and a psyche major, and of course she's a pretty blonde to match her boy-toy. Slim little figure, trying hard to not dress slutty so people will take her and her cause more seriously. Well, I believe in your cause, Natasha. Women have just as much of a right to die horrible deaths as men.

Let's see who's next... It's Ted. Hi, Ted! Looks like Ted is another theater major, except he's not the leading man type. He's tall, skinny, lanky, usually plays the side-kick comic-relief in the school plays. He's got a honker of a nose that would make a toucan jealous, beady little eyes, and a short tuft of red hair. He does stand-up comedy, cheesy magic tricks, blows balloons at kids parties... Wow. I think I've found my next Stuart. This motherfucker is just the type of little cunt whose face just screams out, *Oh please, Mr. Marvin! Make me suffer! Make me suffer soooo bad!* Don't worry, buddy boy, I'll come up with something very special for you.

Next up is Matt. I read up on him and look at his photos, and the only real item of trivia worth noting is that the fucker is in a wheelchair. A high school track star who got in a car crash, and now he's studying office administration. Ooooh, exciting. This dude doesn't drink, doesn't smoke, doesn't eat junk food, doesn't curse, doesn't have any weird hobbies. He's just a nice American boy with plain brown hair, and he's in a wheelchair.

That's it. Not much of a challenge, but oh well. He'll bleed and scream and die the same as anyone else.

I take a delightful sip of brandy and continue.

The next two little sheep share a profile together in the dossier. It looks like Kevin and Sherri are a couple, so much so that they're practically attached at the hip. I guess they're just so similar in every way, there's no point in describing them separately. High school sweethearts now in college together, and they are clearly the resident rebels of the group. Black hair and clothes, leather with studs, piercings, tattoos, bad attitudes... I like them both already. Kevin sees himself as a socialist and anarchist, waving flags and going to rallies and trying to bring down the man. Sherri is just his druggie-slut girlfriend who likes to cut herself and goes along with whatever stupid shit Kevin says or does. Kooky. You both shall die.

Hm, another boring one. Hillary is a short girl with shoulder-length brown hair. Glasses. Pretty plain-looking clothes. Not ugly, but definitely not hot. Philosophy major. Whole lotta good that's gonna do you, honey. Looks like she's a small town girl, grew up very sheltered, and now she's trying to "find herself," whatever that means. So I guess hanging out with a bunch of hippies and sneaking around in an abandoned mental hospital is her way of trying to expand her horizons. Maybe drink a beer, maybe take a puff or two of a joint, maybe even meet a cute boy and get her cherry popped. Good girl wanting to be a bad girl. Take that, daddy!

I turn the page, and take a look at our last contestant, Crystal. Hm, I might just have to bust out some lotion for this one, get my favorite, crusty cum-towel ready. This bitch is smokin' hot. I mean, *woo!* Long, wavy-brown hair, perfect little body, face like an angel, big blue eyes. She could model for lingerie catalogues or do porn, but instead, she seems to be exploring her spiritual side. What a waste. Tarot cards, palm reading, astrology, she's into all that shit. Guess that's how she got the nickname "Crystal Ball."

Looks like this whole excursion to the Chapman Institute was her idea, to try to convene with the spirits trapped there, burn sage, meditate, and align her chakra with the cosmos. Or whatever. In any case, this whole trip is your fault, sweetie. You convinced your friends to go along with this, and it will be my pleasure to make you suffer and die for it.

But first... where's that lotion?

PARTY TIME, baby.

I'm backstage at the Grand Malavista Ampitheater, ready for the clash. Got my old overalls, got my big bare feet, got my bad attitude. Jim is here chomping on a wad of gum, wearing a loud, multi-colored suit that he must think makes him look cool. David Black is here with us backstage as well, donning a slick, black suit, black shirt, black tie, black everything. He's keeping his distance from me at the moment; guess I'm not his favorite person right now.

Three corner-men are assigned to me, standing by with a bottle of water, a bucket, a towel, et cetera. Like

I'm gonna need any of that shit, but this is how the show works, so whatever. All I need is to be let loose to do my thang. I bounce up and down, stretch my neck, warm up my arms. Getting excited. I can hear the crowd cheering and stomping through the walls, shouting my name. I'm a big celebrity now, and I fucking love it.

Other celebs and people of note are milling around backstage. Other boogeymen, rich fat cats, popstars, models, you name it. All the VIPs are here to mingle, slap me on the back, say "go get 'em," and that kind of thing. And that's cool, because I've gotten to meet some dang interesting people. Shit, I look over to my left and there chatting with a few big-wigs and surrounded by his security team, is none other than Satan himself.

I've seen him on the news and in the papers, but nothing could have prepared me for actually seeing him in person. I mean, he's the fucking *devil,* man. And yet... he just looks like some douche. Just a middle-aged bureaucrat in a nondescript suit. A white dude with thinning hair who could stand to lose a few pounds.

He could easily be an insurance salesman, accountant, real estate agent, a local politician advertising by staking little signs on front lawns. He's just some fucking guy. I can't help but be a bit disappointed. He and his posse walk by, and as he sees me, he gives a polite smile and a thumbs-up, and vacantly says, "Hey hey! Alright!" And that's it.

Cunt. Fucking shit down your throat.

I see someone else strutting down the corridor, accompanied by five sleazy whores, decked out in a fluffy-white fur coat, designer shoes, and bling all over his neck and fingers. It's none other than the resident BMC champion himself, Larry "The Snapper" Lindner. He's wearing the gaudiest gold-framed, rose-tinted glasses I've ever seen. For a man whose flesh has been flayed off his skull and who has a steel bear-trap for a mouth, he somehow thinks of himself as a groovy, 1970's disco-pimp.

I turn away from him and stand at the double doors, ready for my music to start to cue my entrance. Jim can't hide his excitement, practically bouncing up and down like a giddy little girl. I roll my eyes and try to ignore him, but this is Jim we're talking about.

"Now remember, just have a good time out there, man!" Jim says, slapping my shoulder. "You are the man! *You* are the man! Nobody does it better! I want you to go in there and show them who you are tonight! You're the biggest! You're the baddest! You're..."

I give Jim my best *shut the fuck up* look, and he gets the hint. My manager extraordinaire clears his throat and goes back to chewing his gum, but now there's another voice calling out to me. My stomach clenches into a knot as I immediately know who it is.

"Well, if it isn't the man of the hour," Larry Lindner quips.

I let out a sigh and turn around.

There he is, a whore on each arm, the other three posing in a semi-circle around him. I'd say he's smiling, but it's kind of hard to tell with those steel jaws bolted over his fucking mouth. Jim holds his arms open like he's greeting an old friend.

"Snapper! Hey man, how you doing? Lookin' good! Y'know, I—"

"Don't talk to me," Larry cuts Jim off, his eyes never leaving mine.

"Okay," Jim mumbles, wisely shutting the fuck up.

"Hewwo, Tsnappa'."

"Melvin, right?" Larry asks, intentionally getting it wrong. Okay, I see how it is. "Well, you certainly are *big*. Good luck out there tonight. You think you can get the job done this time? You'll need to if you think you're gonna take the belt from *me*."

I contain my anger, not giving this clown the satisfaction.

"I'ww do mah bestsh," I say.

"I'm sorry, I didn't catch that."

"He said he'll do his best, Sna—" Jim begins.

"I said shut the fuck up, little man," Larry cuts him off again.

Jim clears his throat and humbly takes a step back.

Larry and I just look at each other, neither breaking eye contact.

"Well," Larry says, "just about that time. I gotta get up to my private box seats. Wouldn't want to miss the show. Good luck out there tonight."

He reaches out to shake my hand. We shake.

We squeeze. Neither of us lets go. It starts to get awkward.

"Thanksth," I finally say, and let go.

Larry smiles—I guess—and puts his arms around his whores, leading them away. "Come on, ladies. Let's go see what big boy can do." And they're gone, Superfly and his bitches, swaggering in unison. Good. Fuck that guy.

"It's time, Mr. Brumlow," a stage hand with a walkie-talkie tells me.

I nod, standing at the double doors, waiting.

My walk-out song begins to play.

"Highway To Hell" by AC/DC. Fuck yeah, dude.

The doors swing open, and the lights of the ampitheater pour in on me. I start to strut into the massive arena, and the crowd goes absolutely fucking batshit crazy. Fireworks explode overhead. I see my name flashing in lights.

"Mar-vin! Mar-vin! Mar-vin!!" I hear them chant.

Following behind me are Jim and my corner-men.

Directly overhead are the eight little hummingbird-fucker-camera-drone-thingies that will follow me to record the slaughter. Up ahead is the stage, and there is that flashy MC—turns out his name is Bruno Bivens, and he's actually really nice. Teaches high school yearbook on the side and does some nice decoupage work—posing around in his shimmery smoking jacket, shouting into the microphone:

"Are you ready for BLOOOOOOD???"

Everyone roars in the affirmative.

"Ladies and gentlemen, MARVIIIIIIIN BRUM-LOOOOOOW!!!"

Jim gives me one last slap on the back and smirks.

"Knock 'em dead, killer. I mean, y'know. Like, literally."

I run up onto the stage and pump my fists in the air.

My adoring fans applaud. Man, I love this job.

"Marvin, are you ready?" Bruno shouts.

I scream and pound my chest like King Kong.

"Then the time... has come... *TO KILL!!!*"

The crowd roars. The buzzer rings and the first period begins.

I step through the veil.

CHAPTER 4

NEVER THOUGHT I'd ever come back to Forest Glen, Illinois, but here I am. I'm standing on a small rural road, cool pavement under my feet. Not a house or a car or a soul in sight. They tend to build places like Chapman off the beaten path a bit; nobody wants a fucking nuthouse in their neighborhood. Nice and secluded, perfect for my purposes. I breathe in the cool air, watching the sun set behind the trees. Pretty soon it'll be dark, and my new friends will arrive.

I know what awaits me down this road. Around the next curve will be the big, wrought-iron gate, then down another stretch is the parking lot, and then finally, the hospital complex. Or what's left of it. Gonna be weird to see this place in ruins. But good-weird, because fuck this place.

So, off I go down the road. I look up, and my eight little hummingbird friends hover around me, following my every move. Five of them suddenly break formation, four zooming ahead to the kill-site, one remaining behind to cover the road. Gotta have cameras on everything so the fans back in Hell can see the action from all angles.

The three remaining drones are assigned to me, following silently as I round the bend.

There's the front gate up ahead. The left side of the wrought-iron frame has been bent and yanked off its hinges long ago. It's covered in rust, graffiti, and overgrown with grass and vines. I see remnants of old beer cans and empty bottles of spray paint. Yup, this has become a haven for local kids, bums, and druggies. The once-polished sign reading "Chapman Institute for the Criminally Insane" now hangs off-kilter and is nearly illegible, covered in dirt and rust.

A tattered front page of The Chicago Tribune has blown against the gate, and I lean in for a closer look. Wednesday, January 21, 1981 is the date. The top headline reads, "Reagan Takes Oath," followed by a second headline reading, "Hostages Safe!" I don't care about either of those things, so I continue up the road.

The large, sprawling parking lot is now completely overgrown and empty. When I finally see the hospital complex, what's left of my jaw drops open. The top half of the main building has been reduced to charred ashes, and the west dormitory has completely burned to the ground. The east dormitory looks untouched, and I can't see the cafeteria/rec center from here. But man, the windows are all shattered, vines have slithered across nearly every surface, graffiti and garbage everywhere... It's a thing of beauty.

Time to explore.

I step through the busted-open front door and into the dark main hall. My feet crunch through layers of dead leaves, broken glass, empty beer cans, and used needles. The last rays of sunlight shine through the broken windows. Smells like dead raccoon and piss. Off in one corner is an old steel barrel punched full of holes where some hobo once made a fire.

I go from room to room; want to get a lay of the land to see what I'm working with before my young friends arrive. The first three floors of the main building were virtually untouched by the fire, but as I climb the stairs to the fourth floor, I start to see charring on the walls, ashes on the floors.

By the time I reach the fifth and final floor, the place is completely gutted, and the entire ceiling has collapsed. Blackened support beams and chunks of wall are strewn everywhere, and the ruined floor is riddled with holes, nearly crumbling under my weight.

Time to get out of here. Nothing interesting up on these top floors anyway, just administrative offices. So I carefully tread back down the steps as my little hummingbird buddies follow. One of the stairs gives way under my feet and I barely catch myself before crashing down through the entire staircase.

I gasp and slap my hand against my chest, breathing a sigh of relief. What the hell, am I afraid of heights or something? I'm fucking immortal, what do I care? Come on, Marvin, don't be a pussy.

I keep moving. It doesn't take long to explore the west dorm. Nothing but blackened chunks of wood, rebar, and the remnants of steel bed frames. No ceiling, tiny pieces of wall and support beams, there is nothing here, just nothing. I'm sure a lot of crazies burned to death here in their beds that night.

The east dorm is untouched. Aside from being dark and filthy, everything is intact. I pass by my old room and feel a chill run through me. Looking at that little steel box, a tiny slot in the door for me to see out of... I don't know if I was insane when I first got here, but I definitely was after I left. That slop they made us eat, those pills... Oh, Doctor Stockton, if I could get my hands on that motherfucker right now!

The cafeteria also looks untouched. I mean, it's filthy, some of the windows are broken and leaves have blown in from outside, but it's more or less intact. Stepping into the dark kitchen, I see much of the same. Dust and cobwebs and mess, but no structural damage.

I open one of the two industrial refrigerators and it's completely empty. I open the other one, and I'm assaulted with piles of mold and festering stink that nearly makes me puke. Yup, somebody left some food in here and now it's all fuzzy and green, mushrooms growing on it, barnacles, fucking stalactites... It's gross.

There are a few utensils scattered here and there, along with some pots and pans, and baking trays. I find an old spatula, a whisk, a can opener, a big carving knife, and a meat cleaver. The blades are a bit rusty, but still good, so I take them with me. If I don't kill at least one person with a big knife, I'll never hear the end of it from Mr. Black.

Out back is what's left of the recreation area. There is a huge lawn, a basketball court, and a flower garden, all surrounded by barbed-wire fencing, and all completely overgrown with vines and weeds. I see more empty steel trash cans where bums and local kids have made campfires, and all the beer cans and food wrappers they left behind. Two wild dogs are scavenging back here, and when they hear me, they bolt off through a hole in the fence and vanish into the surrounding woods. I continue to stroll around until I hear a sound that stops me in my tracks. A sound I loathe, a sound I detest...

Pop music.

My heart flutters like a little boy waking up on Christmas morning; Santa has come to bring me my presents! I drop what I'm doing and hurry back to the main building. Shuffling through the dark, trying not to step on all the dried leaves and items of garbage everywhere, I make my way through the corridors until I reach the front entrance. The sound of that horrible music grows louder, and I hear footsteps, engines idling, and youthful laughter.

I peek through a broken window and there they are. Johnny, Natasha, Hillary, and Matt are gathered around an old, red VW Bug—there's apparently always someone with a red VW Bug—with Hillary helping Matt scoot into his wheelchair. Pulling up behind them is a small Toyota pickup truck, battered and scratched and dented and covered in stickers, with an entirely different kind of insufferable music blasting out: Punk Rock.

The truck squeals to a halt in the gravel, and its occupants hop out. Kevin and Sherri and Crystal and Ted. *Crystal*, mmmm... From the look in Ted's eyes, he wants a piece of that hippy-dippy-hottie, and from the look in her eyes, she couldn't care less about his carrot-topped scarecrow ass.

"Heeeeeeey, baby!"

"Woo!"

"Let's get this party rockin'!"

I hear them all hooting and shouting, high-fiving, and joking around as they convene outside the cars. Actor-boy Johnny hefts a cooler from his trunk, and his hottie—I think she's his—girlfriend Natasha pulls out a rucksack and a big cardboard box. Looks like they've come prepared for their little adventure, or so they think.

Sherri straps on a backpack stitched together with safety pins and covered in punk-band patches and stickers. She scoops up a small boombox (also covered in stickers) and a flashlight. Kevin dons a backpack and a flashlight as well. The two anti-capitalism wannabe-rockers huddle together, and he gives her a kiss with his pierced lips, their acne-riddled faces rubbing together. Gross.

"I can't believe we're actually doing this," Johnny says.

"Aww, what's the matter, Johnny?" Natasha teases. "You scared?"

"Shut up," he says, wrapping his arms around Natasha, tickling her and making her giggle. Okay yeah, they do seem to be an item.

"It is pretty creepy," Hillary says.

"Don't worry," Matt snickers. "If any ghosts show up, I'll kick their ass."

I bet he almost could. Wheelchair Boy's got some guns on him, and he knows it. His t-shirt is a size too small so he can emphasize every flex. Probably one of those Special Olympics fuckers. Hillary blushes and rests her hand on Matt's shoulder, practically drooling. Okay, so she's got the hots for Wheelie, he's in a wheelchair... I wonder if I can find some cool way to work these elements together into their murders.

"It's nothing to joke about, Matt," Crystal says. "A lot of people died here. I'm already sensing a very heavy energy in this place. I'm going to try and make contact with any spirits who may still be trapped here, and I need you to take it seriously."

Matt rolls his eyes.

"I'm with ya, Crystal," Ted snarks, slipping on a cheap pair of Groucho Marx glasses with the big nose. "I'll take it seriously."

"I think it's hot," Sherri says, eyeballing the place with a twisted smile. "All the death, and decay, and filth... Fuckin' turns me on."

Hm. Now this chick, I kind of like.

"That's my girl!" Kevin says proudly, sparking up a cigarette.

"Seriously, guys," Hillary says, looking around at her friends, "what if there's like, homeless people in there, or something? What if some of the patients who survived stayed here, or...?"

Johnny smiles with an annoying level of self-confidence and says, "There's nobody here, Hillary. And just in case, I have this." He reaches into his car and pulls out a wooden Louisville Slugger.

"And I have this," Kevin says, whipping out a butterfly knife, flipping it around and showing it off.

"And I have *this!*" Ted whoops, waving his hand and suddenly, a bouquet of prop magic-flowers pops out of his sleeve. He offers the flowers to Crystal, bobbing his eyebrows up and down. "M'lady?"

She just looks at him.

I cannot wait to murder this fucking kid.

Natasha curiously steps forward, sweeping her flashlight across the front of the building. I hunker down behind the window frame so she can't see me.

"Let's just start bringing the stuff in, you guys," Natasha says, seemingly taking command. "We'll find a place to chill, explore around... but be careful. Nobody goes off alone anywhere. I'm more worried about the ceiling caving in on us or falling through a rotten floor than getting attacked by bums or ghosts."

Okay, so she's the smart one. Or at least she thinks she is. I'll come up with a fitting demise for you, blondie.

It looks like everyone is falling in line and following Natasha's lead, gathering up their gear to carry inside. Guess I'll retreat into the shadows for a while. I'll let them wander around, do their thing, and then when the time is right, Splatter City.

CHAPTER 5

I HATE THIS PART.

It's so boring. There's no death, no blood, no beauti-ful, agonized screaming, just... waiting. I guess I could storm in there right now, hack everybody up, and just get it over with. But that's not what the fans want; I'm supposed to make a meal of this. Pick them off one at a time, ratchet up the suspense, give the good people of Hell their money's worth, that's how you win the belt.

But that means I have to wait around and listen to these fuckers *talking*, and watch them dance around like clowns to this puke they call music. I guess it's supposed to enhance the drama for the fans, to get to know the poor victims, where they're from, what they're like... I don't care. Call me shallow, but I don't need to know how Johnny came to be the way he is, or how Hillary is feeling on the inside. I'm just interested in seeing how her insides look when they splash down around my bare feet.

Right now, they're all carrying in their boxes and bags, and are using the main entrance hall as their base camp. Johnny is setting up their little makeshift bar, while Natasha lights a shitload of candles and sets up two electric lanterns. Matt and Hillary are getting to know each other and talking about some stupid shit, while Kevin and Sherri are already hitting the booze. Ted is trying to entertain Crystal, who is obviously preoccupied with projecting her aura into the cosmos, aligning her chi with the spirits... or something. Take the hint, Ted.

"Wow, the energy is really heavy in here, you guys," Crystal says with her eyes closed, holding her hands out to sense the vibes. I'm sensing many entities, so much pain..."

"I read about this place a lot during my Criminal Psychology class last semester," Natasha adds. "It's incredible how many serial killers and delusional psychopaths were sent here. Multiple personality disorders, szcizophrenics, you name it. This is where they sent the worst of the worst."

"This is where they sent Brumlow, right?" Matt asks.

Natasha nods.

"Oh, shit! Maybe we can make contact with him!" Kevin says.

"No," Natasha shakes her head. "He didn't die in the fire. He was released years earlier, and that's when he began his killing spree. The public uproar over them letting him out was the reason they burned this place down. The angry townspeople grabbed their torches and pitchforks... and the rest is history."

From the grunt that Kevin makes, he sounds disappointed. Don't worry, buddy. If you want to make contact with me, I think that can be arranged.

"Well, whatever spirits are here, we reach out to them with this," Crystal says, pulling a Ouija board from her bag and starting to set it up. "But I need everyone to be quiet, and to take this seriously." She shoots a look at Ted.

"Yeah yeah, okay," the carrot-top bean pole rolls his eyes and agrees.

"Well, I want to take a look around first, you guys," Johnny says, pointing his flashlight around. "Don't you want to check this place out?"

"Yeah!" Kevin and Sherri say in unison.

Through my limited vantage point, I can see my darling little sheep milling about, some setting up their stuff, others starting to peak into side rooms and dark corridors. But the way this place is laid out, I can't get too close by looking around corners and through broken windows. One of these fuckers is going to see me soon unless I either hide farther away, or duck behind the veil for a while.

I opt for the latter. All I have to do is step through the veil, and I'm in the world between worlds. I can come right up to you and you wouldn't even know it. I can walk through walls, be like a ghost, then whenever I feel like it, pop right back in. It's so easy, it almost takes the fun out of the kill. Almost.

Like a big curtain, I split open the veil and step on through, vanishing from the Earthly dimension. Now here I am, still in the same room, but everything is cold and foggy. I can still see and hear my prey, but it's through a haze. Everything is dream-like behind the veil, a plane of existence that's neither here nor there. So I smile and move at ease, not needing to tiptoe around anymore.

I come in to get a better look at the kids. Johnny and

Natasha have started down one dark hallway, flashlights in hand, while Matt and Hillary are exploring further into the main entrance hall. Kevin and Sherri have sparked up a blunt and seem to have no intention of getting up from their cozy-little spot.

Meanwhile, Crystal sets up her Ouija board and starts burning sage and incense, while Ted attempts to help her, but succeeds only in entertaining himself. So now all I need to do is wait for one of them to venture off on their own, and *bam*, they're mine.

Then out of nowhere, I hear a voice that I never thought I'd hear again in a million fucking years, let alone right here, right now...

"Marvin?"

What the fuck? I turn around and see a crusty, blackened, charred figure limping towards me through the haze. He looks like something I'd scrape off the bottom of my convection oven after years of use. He's definitely a man, or what's left of one.

His right arm is missing, and most of his skin has become a husk of black tar and charcoal. But here and there, I start to see patches of flesh that haven't been burned to a crisp. The left half of his face is mostly unharmed, including a vibrant green eye, and a small surviving tuft of curly blonde hair. No way, it can't be.

"Marvin, is that you?" the burnt figure asks again.

"Who'sth dat?" I ask, absolutely baffled.

"It's me, Hank!" I see the charred flesh on his skull pull into a crunchy smile.

"Hang? I don' bewiebe id!" I slur in excitement. Right there before my eyes is good 'ol Hank Whittaker.

He's looked better. Last time I saw Hank, we were both patients within these walls. "Whad da fug ah' you doin' heah, Hang?" I ask as I shake his one good hand.

"What am *I* doin' here?" Hank says with a chuckle. "I've been here since I died in the fire. I'm a fuckin' ghost!"

"No shid? Aw, thad thucksth."

"Yeah, man. What about your big ass? What are *you* doin' here?"

I shrug and smile. "Oh, jusp heah ta kiw 'dese kibs."

"Right on," Hank nods. "Hey fellas, look who's here!"

I look around, and creeping out of the mists and shadows, there are more of them. Mangled shapes that used to be men. Some are even crispier than Hank, while others have minimal burns and wounds. Now they're all trapped here together, a bunch of spectral psychopaths, rapists, and killers, spending their eternities together in purgatory. I start to recognize faces, though I can't remember all their names.

"Who dat?" one of the burnt husks asks.

"It's Marvin!" Hank says cheerfully.

"Marvin? Marvin Brumlow?"

"Hey, everybody look! It's Marvin!"

"Marvin! Hey, man!"

One by one, they all come forward to greet me. It's good to see them, sort of. I mean, some of these dudes are nothing more than blackened bones and it's kind of awkward. What am I supposed to say, *Hey man, lookin' good*? If I had a heart, I'd feel sad for these guys.

"Hey, guysth," I say politely.

"Marvin's here to kill these asshole kids!" Hank says.

"Whoa! Cool!"

"Far out!"

One of the char-broiled corpses appears to be fervently massaging himself under his pants, looking into the other room at the lovely young ladies on display. If I remember correctly, this guy's name is Neiman? Neimar? Anyway, he was a serial rapist who became a killer before he was finally caught. I guess even after being horribly burned and killed, he still can't stop whackin' off.

"Oh man, look at the brunette, man!" Neiman says, trembling. "The one with the Ouiji board! So sweet and young..."

"Easy there, buddy," another ghost says with a laugh.

"Yeah, you ain't getting none of that, Neiman!" says another.

"Fuck you guys," Neiman says. "Ohhh, the things I would do..."

As Neiman continues to caress his flame-broiled weiner, the others laugh and chat happily. Hank slaps me on the shoulder, a sincere smile on his face.

"It's good to see you, man," Hank says.

"You too," I say. "I can' tawk fuh lowng, cus' I godda' kiw 'dese kibs. It'sh mah yob. Bu' I'm sowwy you gob sthuck heah. Thad thucksth."

"Ah, no worries, man. We just hang out, do whatever. A lot of people come in here to squat for a while, so we get to watch them. There's always some bums or drug addicts or somethin', and we kinda like to just fuck with 'em, y'know? Hell, there's three of 'em right now squattin' in the east dorm."

My posture straightens up a bit. That got my attention.

"I wasth in theah justhp a ppfew minudsth ago," I say. "I didn' thsee anyone in theah."

"Oh sure, they have their hiding spots. Anytime they hear somebody coming, they scoot and hide like cockroaches. But they're in there, all right."

Hmm. I can't just have three random people roaming around during my happy-happy fun time. They could spoil everything. And of course, the fans back in Hell don't care who I kill, they just want to see blood and guts. So yeah, fuck it, I'll go get them out of the way first.

"Coo'. Fthanksth, Hang. Thing' I'ww go pay 'dose bumsth a 'bisit."

"Ooh! Can I watch you kill 'em, Marvin?" One roasted fucker asks.

"Me too! Me too!"

I shrug. Why not? No matter where I go, everyone wants to watch me kill. Plus, these poor ol' boys deserve a little show. Hank slaps me on the shoulder and laughs as I start on down the hall to find these squatters.

"Have fun, buddy," Hanks says. "I'll keep an eye on your kids for ya."

"Mmmm, yeahhh," Neiman coos, stroking himself. "I'll keep an eye on *her*."

"Yeeaahhh," several other charred ghosts murmur in agreement.

I snort and shake my head at the undead perv. But that's fine, who am I to talk? I'm about to go hack up three pour souls simply because they are here. Not worried about my primary targets at the moment. They're not going anywhere. Let them explore for a while and fuck around, that's fine. I'll be back.

This will be a little warm-up, an unexpected bonus for the fans. Going above and beyond, that's how you become the champ. This whole thing's just a bullshit popularity contest anyway, and for the first time in my life—er, afterlife—I can be the best at something. The most popular.

So, suck it, Larry. I'm coming to take what you got. I'm gonna hit every target in spectacular fashion, and then some. I *will* be the champion.

CHAPTER 6

GOTTA MAKE this quick and quiet.

Killing three bums wasn't part of the initial plan, so I have to be careful. If they start screaming, running around and crying for help, that will alert my eight young friends. And if they get scared off and escape... well, let's just say my star power and street cred in Hell will go right out the fucking window. So in order to remain stealthy for now, I remain behind the veil.

I approach the east dorm. Behind me, a few of my extra-crispy old buddies follow to watch the show. In the air around me, three of the hummingbird cameras float and follow my every move. The fans are all watching back home, and I'd better have some gore on my hands before the first period is over, or they'll be pissed.

This is the second time tonight I've walked through the main hall of the east dorm, but this time, I'm behind the veil. I'm invisible, a ghost. No creaky floorboards to alert anyone of my presence. And sure enough, I see movement and light at the end of the hall. It's coming from the recreation area, where we would all get to watch TV, play ping-pong, sit around in a circle and have our bullshit group therapy sessions.

I see steam rising and smell some pork and beans. Looks like our squatters got themselves a bunson burner. As I get closer, I finally see them, three shabby figures huddled around on the couches, enjoying their little makeshift nest. One older guy stirring the pot of chow is the portrait of a quintessential hobo, down to the scraggly beard and torn rags for clothing. The other two look like a younger couple, hippies with no marketable job skills who ran out of things to protest in college. Now they're crouched together in squalor, sharing a crack pipe, living the dream.

The girl takes a big hit of rock and starts coughing uncontrollably. Her boyfriend slaps her back, trying to help, but she just continues hacking her fucking lungs out.

The old hobo is visibly annoyed.

"Shh! Will you keep it down?" he hisses.

"Oh come on, man. Nobody can hear us," the boyfriend says. "Those kids are in the other building."

"Yeah, and if they come in here?"

"Then we just hide again. Or you smash 'em with your fuckin' skillet. Chill, man. It'll be all right."

The old bum grumbles and resumes stirring his pork and beans. He does have a small cast-iron skillet, which will make for a nice murder weapon, I must say. The girl finally stops coughing and her loving beau takes the pipe so he can have the next hit. He coughs it out and they start laughing and giggling and kissing, and Old Hobo Guy looks as annoyed about it as me.

Okay, now that I've zeroed in on my targets, I'm gonna step back into the physical world. I pick a spot just around the corner from where they are, behind a wall, and open up the veil. Once I'm back, I feel the difference in the atmosphere. The air is warmer, more humid. The fogginess behind the veil is gone. Right away, I'm hit by the pungent smell in the room. Boy, the aroma of pork n' beans n' crack is a difficult thing to describe.

I hide here for a minute in the dark, listening to them, waiting for my chance. Ideally, I want to get them separated, and I want to do this as quietly as possible. Which is too bad, because all the ideas I have involve methods of murder that will cause the most horrible, delightful, blood-curdling screaming a human being can produce. Quick and quiet, Marvin. Okay, I'll try.

A couple minutes later, I get my chance.

Old Hobo Guy is grumbling again about the two lovebirds getting high and being annoying. I hear the sound of him scraping the pork n' beans into a bowl and stomping away, muttering about how he'd rather eat by himself, something like that. Good. You're up first.

His old ass ambles out of the rec room and down the dark hall, scooping food into his mouth. I slowly lurch out of my hiding spot and follow him. He goes into the main corridor with all the old patient rooms, most of the doors still ajar. I watch him pick a room and step in. I hear him plop onto the old, rusty springs of the cot, continuing to munch away. I move in closer.

Closer. I'm just outside the room now.

Hmm, how should I do this? I don't want to go in there; kind of promised myself I'd never go back in one of these fucking cells again. So, I'll get him to come out. An easy solution quickly presents itself. Mixed in with the leaves and rubbish and filth on the floor is what looks like a broken piece of a lunch tray. I pick it up and throw it.

The plastic shard of garbage clatters to the floor, and the sound echoes down the hall. I can't see my old friend in there, but I can just imagine that sent a shiver up his spine and his body is all tensed in fear right now. I look at the open doorway, with the large steel door hanging open, and see nothing but pitch black inside.

I wait just behind the door for a minute. Another minute. Come on, fucker. Come out and take a look. Don't you want to know what that was? Another minute. Okay, let's try this again. I pick up another piece of trash and flick it across the room. It clacks against a wall. This time, I hear a muffled gasp coming from inside the cell. Come on, asshole. Come take a look.

I throw another piece of trash, a crumpled paper cup. The sound echoes down the hall. The old hobo's breathing is getting heavy, and I'm sure his heart is pounding hard as fuck too. Finally, I hear him whisper —

"Guys? Is that you?"

Nope, it's not your crackhead friends.

"Guys? Come on, quit foolin' around..."

I flick a filthy old pen this time. I'm going fishing. Gotta be patient when you're fishing. If my daddy ever taught me anything at all, other than how to be violent and cruel, it was fishing. Just be patient, and the fish will take the bait. And of course, Old Hobo Guy finally takes the bait, and pokes his head out into the hall.

"Guys?" he calls out.

WHAM!!!

All I have to do is kick the door shut, and it smashes

the old fucker's head like a watermelon. Brains and skull and eyeballs explode everywhere, and I get the added bonus of the sound getting nicely muffled. Instead of a loud, metallic *clang* alerting everyone in Illinois, there's just a muted, meaty *crunch*.

I hear his body on the other side of the door slide down, and I enjoy watching just how much blood gushes out when a man's head explodes. It's so deep, and red, and thick... Mmm, nice. *Woo!* Okay, not bad. Pretty good one. I look up, and all eight of my little hummingbird friends are hovering around me, getting the action from every angle.

The crowd in the arena is no doubt losing their shit right now. Up on the huge screens, they'll be watching slow-motion replays of that moneyshot from all eight angles. Splat. *Mar-vin! Mar-vin! Mar-vin!* I give the flying cameras a cocky nod, pounding my fist against my chest. That's right, motherfuckers, *I* am the man.

Time for Tweedle Dee and Tweedle Dumb.

I walk back down the corridor, my bare feet crunching through the dead leaves. As I come back into the rec room, I wipe all the shit off the bottoms of my feet. Don't need them hearing me. Creeping further into the dim room, I hear them up ahead. Sounds like they're fooling around. I peek around the corner and there they are.

They're on the ratty-old couch, her on top. Her shirt is off, skirt hiked up, rank panties pulled aside to let loverboy in. She's grinding on him, and there are the tell-tale sickly, droopy, ugly titties of a crackhead. Pale, filthy, acne everywhere. Both their eyes are sunken and glazed-over. So pathetic. Just wearily going at it, no energy, no zest... Let me fix that.

I step out from the behind the wall and approach them.

They don't notice me. I come in closer.

Finally, I'm standing right over them, and Loverboy opens his eyes. He sees me. He blinks, his face expressionless. He's so fried, he doesn't even have the sense to be afraid. Time to put them both out of their misery, but first, I have to show them how to fuck good and hard.

I lunge in and grab them both by the backs of their necks. There is a split second of shock and terror in their eyes, and it looks like they're just about to start screaming. Nope, can't let that happen.

SMASH!! SMASH!! SMASH!!

I just start bashing their faces and bodies into each other. The key here with this kind of kill is to use only juuuust enough strength. If I really slammed them both face-to-face at full strength, they'd just explode in a fountain of gore on the very first strike. But if I use juuuust enough strength, I can prolong their suffering and make it more enjoyable for the fans.

So, after the first three blows, they're both still alive. Their noses and orbital sockets are shattered, and their teeth and jaws are pulverized. But they're alive. They're both gasping and choking on blood and teeth, but still conscious. So I keep going.

SMASH!! SMASH!! SCRUNCHH!!

After a few more low-strength strikes, I can feel their skulls really start to break down, their rib cages caving in, their blood and goo spraying everywhere. Oh yeah, they are far past conscious at this point. I'd be surprised if either still has a pulse, but let me just finish this up and put a nice bowtie on it.

Enough of this low-strength shit. I really apply pressure, smashing them repeatedly into each other, and mashing and grinding their brains and bones and guts together like I'm making spicy meatballs.

Now you little bitches are fucking *hard*.

I toss what's left of them aside, and it splats onto the filthy linoleum. Unsurprisingly, I'm completely covered in blood. I look down at the front pocket of my overalls, and one of the girl's eyeballs is floating around in there, looking up at me. I toss that shit away and start wiping myself down. Their raggedy clothes are nearby, so I scoop them up to wipe as much of this shit off myself as I can.

I get most of the schmutz off my face and arms, but my overalls are just soaked in it. That's fine. As long as the good people watching are enjoying themselves, that's all that matters. I look up at one of the hummingbird fuckers hovering across from me, and flex my bicep for it.

Enjoy, you sick bastards.

The small frying pan is still on the burner, a good bit of pork n' beans sizzling in it. Shit, I forgot to use the skillet to kill them. Oh well, I'll use it on Ted. Yeah, that'll be good. So I scoop it up, find a fork, and dig in as I head back to introduce myself to my new friends.

Mm, tasty!

CHAPTER 7

BY THE TIME I get back, it looks like the party is well underway. Our group of daring young explorers has the main lobby all decked out as their little lounge area. A shitload of candles are now lit and placed all over the room—great idea, burn the rest of the place down!—and everybody has a good buzz going. Sherri is playing more of that new wave punk shit through her crappy boombox. Matt and Hillary are sharing a pleasant drink and chatting. Crystal has finished setting up her Ouija board, putting it on top of a box with a tie-dyed silk scarf draped over it.

"Okay, guys. You ready?" Crystal says.

The others mutter and begin to fall in, sitting down in a circle around the board game. Johnny and Natasha happily come over, as do Matt and Hillary.

"Come on, Sherri," Crystal says. "Can you turn the music off, please?"

Punky Bitch rolls her eyes and turns off the boombox with a snarl.

"Let's go, babe," Kevin says, putting his arm around her. "This'll be fun."

They join the others and prepare to contact the other

side. None of them has a clue how close they are to actually *being* on the other side. I chuckle and watch, shaking my head. This is going to be fun, but for some reason, I'm starting to feel like something's missing.

"Now, everybody just close your eyes and be quiet," Crystal says. "We have to take this seriously or it won't work. What we're going to do is we all reach in and touch the pointer, then we ask a question. Then, make sure you don't consciously try to move the pointer. Just let your fingers touch it lightly, and see where it starts to move."

Kevin rips out the loudest belch he can muster.

"Hahaaa, good one!" Matt says, clapping his hands.

As the others chuckle, Crystal is getting pissed.

"Come on, you guys!"

Johnny sees her frustration and decides to come to the rescue.

"Guys, guys, come on," he says. "Give it a chance."

They continue to argue and bicker, and I can't help but laugh.

Still, I feel like something's missing.

"Shut up, you guys," Natasha says. "This could be cool."

"Look, we didn't come here to talk to Elvis, dude," Sherri slurs. "We came here to get fuuuuuucked up!"

"Yeah, man!" Kevin backs up his girl. "Where's the fuckin' tequila, anyway?"

"It'll be here soon," Johnny says. "Ted said he'd be right back with the rest of the stuff. Would you just relax?"

Oh, no. Wait a second. Where's Ted?

That's what's missing, Ted! Where is he? He didn't... oh, shit.

I turn and run for the door. Oh, no. Oh, no no no no no. Please don't be gone, please don't be gone! I burst through the doors and stomp out into the front courtyard. The shitty pickup truck remains parked where it was before, but the VW Bug is gone.

Ted is gone.

No! Fuck fuck fuck! He must have made a run for the liquor store or something. Damn it, this is my fault. I completely forgot to disable the two vehicles. I should've slashed the tires or maybe yanked their spark plugs, stranding them here. Shit! How could I forget? Now I'm standing here with a cast-iron skillet in my hand, and no redheaded scarecrow to beat to death with it.

I grumble and kick at the gravel, throw the skillet down in frustration, stomping around and having a mini tantrum. But I can't beat myself up too much. Sounds like he just went out to get some booze, and he'll be right back. Relax, Marvin. In the meantime, I go to the pickup, yank up the hood, and rip the spark plugs out. There. Now I can continue with things as planned, and whenever Ted gets back, I'll deal with him too.

So I head back inside.

"CALLING any spirits who may be here, we come in peace."

Crystal leads the group in the hokey seance thing. Kevin and Hillary are the only ones sitting back and watching, while the others all have their fingertips touching the pointer on the Ouija board.

"Are there are spirits who wish to make contact?" Crystal continues. "If so, please move the pointer to 'yes.' We would love to talk with you."

Natasha, Johnny, Matt, and Hillary keep concentrating. Kevin sparks up a joint and passes it to Sherri. I hang back and watch from my vantage point, hidden in the shadows, curious. This is all bullshit, right? Crystal keeps calling out for an answer, and they wait. Finally, something starts to happen.

"Look! It's moving!" Hillary says.

The others perk up, getting excited as the little pointer thing does appear to start wiggling around. Slowly, it slides over to point at the word 'yes' on the board.

"You're moving it yourself," someone says.

"I am not!"

"Johnny, stop it!"

"Don't move it, just touch it lightly. Let it move itself."

"I know, I know."

"Stop moving it!"

They bicker and squabble, but the pointer continues to move.

"What's your name?" Crystal asks.

The pointer slides around, selecting the letters B-E-M.

"B-E-M?" Natasha asks. "You mean BEN? Is your name Ben?"

The pointer slowly makes its way over to say 'yes.' The group reacts with amazement, except for Kevin and Sherri, who are more interested in getting high and feeling each other up. Shit, can't blame them. Crystal proceeds with more questions, as excitement and fear grows in the others' eyes.

"Thank you for joining us, Ben. Were you a patient here?"

The pointer slides to 'yes.'

"Did you die here?"

Yes.

This is all bullshit, right? Well shit, let me check.

I open up the veil and step on through to the other side. There's that cold air again, that mist. And sure enough, there's Hank, Neiman, and some of the other guys standing around, watching the proceedings. They're all snickering and making fun of the dumb kids, except for Neiman, who has his eyes locked on Crystal and is furiously masterbating. They turn and nod politely as they see me step through.

"Hey, man," Hank says.

"Hey guysth," I say. "Isth dat you guysth doin' dat?"

"Pssh. Nah, dude," Hank chuckles. "Those things don't work. These dumb shits are just moving it around themselves." The others laugh.

Neiman reaches out with the hand not stroking his oven-roasted prick, trying to touch Crystal's face. Obviously, he's a ghost so his hand just passes right through her head. Poor girl has no clue that there's a burned, spectral rapist-murderer literally trying to grope her from beyond the grave.

"Mmmm, *Crystal*," Neiman mutters, licking his lips. "Ohhh, little grrrrrl..."

"Yeah, I'd like to get me a piece of that too," another crispy ghoul says.

I chuckle and shake my head, waving again to the group.

"Okay, thanksth guysth," I say. "Tsee ya!"

I step back through the veil and am back in the physical world. Ugh, I think I like purgatory better. At least behind the veil it doesn't *stink*. Whatever, I continue to watch the charade. I wonder if any of them are intentionally moving the pointer thing, or if it's all subconscious.

"How did you die?" Crystal asks.

The pointer magically spells out F-I-R-E.

Hillary looks visibly shaken. "I'm scared, you guys..."

"Don't be afraid," Matt says, putting his hand on hers. "I'm here."

Crystal persists, "Are you trapped here, Ben? Are you unable to cross over to the other side?"

Yes.

"It's okay, Ben," she continues. "You don't have to stay in this place. Your spirit is free now. Just walk into the light, Ben. Walk into the light..."

Kevin sticks his tongue out and blasts a fart sound.

The tension is cut and everybody laughs. Everyone except Crystal.

"God damn it, Kevin! You're such a jerk!"

"Oh, lighten up."

"If you're not gonna take this seriously, then get out of here!"

"Hey, that's fine with me, *Crystal Ball*. This shit is

lame anyway," Kevin says, staggering to his feet and yanking Sherri up with him.

"I don't want to do this anymore either," Hillary whimpers. "I'm scared."

"You guys all suck, you know that?" Crystal sulks.

Natasha chuckles and slaps her friend on the back, standing up to stretch.

"Relax, Crystal," she says. "Maybe we should take a break anyway. Wait for Ted to get back. Do our own thing for a while?"

"Yeah," Johnny says. "I want to explore anyway. I mean, we got all night."

"Fine with me," Matt says, then turns to Hillary. "Want to go for a little spin?"

Everyone seems to murmur in agreement, standing up and stretching and getting ready to go their own ways. I agree. It's definitely a good idea for you all to split up. What's the worst that could happen?

"Come on, babe," Sherri says, "let's go get us a nice dirty, spooky spot."

Sherri scoops up her boom box and punches the play button, and more of that new wave punk shit comes puking out. Kevin drapes an arm around her neck and begins to lead her away, a sleazy, twisted smile on his pimply face.

"Fuck yeah, dude," Kevin says. "I got a salty load in 'dese nuts, and it ain't gonna blow itself, y'know?" Classy, Kevin.

Sid and Nancy drunkenly stumble away to find themselves a little love nest, and it looks like the others are doing the same.

"Okay, guys," Johnny says. "Remember your flashlights, and let's all meet back here in an hour. Okay?"

"Yeah, yeah."

"Yes, mother."

And that's it. They disperse.

Hmmm, who should I kill next?

CHAPTER 8

I THINK I'm running out of time in the first period, so I feel like I have to get at least one more good kill in before then. Sure, I just offed the squatters in the east building, but those were bonus points. I need to start picking off my primary targets, so I take a minute to contemplate who should get it next.

Johnny, Natasha, and Crystal look like they're heading out back to explore the yard, while Matt and Hillary are off to check out the ruins that once was the west dorm. Which leaves my two favorite counter-culture rebels, Kevin and Sherri, who are off to the east dorm, their shitty music echoing down the dark, grungy hall. That's where I left the bodies of those three bums, so I definitely don't want them finding that mess, then screaming and running for help.

Looks like Kevin and Sherri win the prize.

Rather than following behind them, I sneak outside through the front door and loop around to the other end of the east dorm. There's a side entrance I can get in through where they won't see me from the main hall. So I go back outside, pleasant breeze on my skin, a full moon peeking through some clouds. Ahhh, this is nice. I crunch through some dried leaves and overgrowth, finding the side door ajar.

It's the entrance through the kitchen, which leads into the cafeteria, which leads into the old patient rooms of the east dorm. Glancing over at the rec room, I see the bodies of the two crackhead lovers I left on the couch. I say bodies, but it really looks more like a big pile of sloppy joes. And here I am, off to murder another couple of filthy, drug-addict kids.

Into the main hall now, and the first thing that catches my eye is the pile of rubble that used to be Old Hobo Guy's head. There it is, at the base of the crack in the door frame, drying on the linoleum. Might as well try to clean that mess up a little, make it less visible, so I open the door and bit and sweep the larger chunks of it back into the room. There's still a good splat of blood on the floor, but whatever, it's not like I'm gonna fucking *mop*; just want to get the big stuff out of the way.

I proceed down the hall, but I don't see any lights, no shadowy figures looking around. However, I do hear the muffled sounds of that shit music coming through the walls. Creeping past each room, I peek in and see nothing but empty cubicles. They're not in one of the rooms. So then where the... Ah! The shower room. That's on the next level up.

Okay, I hustle over to the staircase and climb up to the second floor. There are some empty offices, the laundry room, and then towards the end of the corridor, the shower room. I hear that boombox coming from inside, echoing off the tile surfaces all around. Then I hear Kevin and Sherri talking and giggling about something, but it's too faint to tell what they're saying.

I poke my head in and start tip-toeing into the shower room. There are sinks and toilets to the left, and on the right is the row of shower stalls. They're each divided by a tile wall, about five feet high, and no doors or curtains. No privacy in this place, that's for sure. I creep in closer, seeing lights and movement coming from one of the stalls. Bad Punk music. Yup, I've found them.

"Oh yeah, baby," Sherri groans. "Treat me like a little fucking whore!"

"Yeah, that's it, bitch! You like that?"

I move in closer. Their two flashlights are on the floor, along with the boombox, which is blasting out some shitty song about...what's he saying? Taking a ride? I don't know, it just sounds like some drunk teenager complaining. I hear the sounds of Kevin and Sherri kissing, groping, pushing each other against the walls. I suddenly see Sherri's shirt fly out of the stall and land on the floor in front of me.

"Oh, yes! I love it! Slap me! Choke me! Spit on me! Cum on my face and then fucking piss all over me!" Jesus, this bitch is rancid.

"Yeah, that's my nasty little bitch," Kevin says, followed by a hard slap. "You want to be dirty for me? You want to be real dirty?"

"Oh, yes! Yes!"

"Well, how about I rub your face into this filthy fucking wall?"

I hear the sound of him pressing her cheek against the

grungy tile surface and wiping it all around. "You like that, you fucking *pig?*"

"Oh God, yes! Yes, I love it! *I love it!*"

I turn to see my invisible, flying camera friends hovering around. I know the fans back in Hell are loving this shit. All I can do is shake my head and shrug. This is too much, even for me. I hear them slapping against the walls in there, making all kinds of weird sounds I can't even identify.

"Okay, get on your knees and open your mouth, bitch!"

"Oh, yes *sir!*"

I see her knees hit the floor through the gap at the bottom of the stall partition, then the sound of his zipper. She goes to work. I think what I'm going to do is sneak into the stall next to them, then wait for the right moment to make my move. I begin to creep forward.

"Oh, yeah!—*glug glug glug*—Fuck my face!—*glug glug glug*—Fuck it and blow that big load, baby!—*glug glug glug!*"

They keep going and I make it to the next stall over, crouching down and walking on the balls of my feet. I'd like to stab through the wall and into Kevin's back, but I don't think this knife will make it. I can, however, reach over the top of the wall and slit his throat. Hm, not a bad idea. In fact, if I wait until his moment of orgasmic pleasure... oh boy, this is gonna be good.

Sherri continues to suck and spit and slobber, and Kevin is egging her on. He's groaning and squirming, nearing the height of ecstasy. She's begging for a hot, sloppy mess all over her face. I peek over the wall, raising the knife.

"Oh, God... Oh, God! You want that big load on your face, bitch?"

"*Glug glug glug*—Oh, yeah!"

Kevin's getting close.

"Oh, yeah... I'm gonna cum!"

I get ready.

"*Ohhhhh, I'm cumming!!*"

Now! I reach over the wall, wrap my huge hand over Kevin's entire face and yank his head back against the wall. With one quick swipe, I slash his throat open.

I hear Kevin buckle and kick and groan as his blood sprays from his carotid artery. Little Sherri, bless her heart, feels the hot splashing of her boyfriend's blood all over her, and doesn't have a clue what's going on yet.

"Ohhhh, *wow!!*" Sherri shouts. "That's a fucking *lot*, baby! Oh my *God!!* It just keeps coming! Oh God, it's so fucking *hot!* It's so... it's... it's... What the fuck?"

Yes, that's right, dummy. That's blood. And this is my cue. I step out of the stall I'm in and cross in front of the door, finally getting a good look at the lovely couple. Sherri is looking down at herself, wondering why she's drenched in blood. The last bit of life drains out of Kevin's throat, and his body drops limp to the floor while she sits there in shock. Slowly, her eyes look up at me.

I fill the doorway. The gory knife drips in my hand.

I'm a monstrous beast, a slimy, hairy redneck, sweaty and dirty. Dried blood all over me. The lower half of my face like something from the butcher shop. I am a walking nightmare sent from Hell to kill you, little girl.

"Y-You killed Kevin..." she stammers.

That's right, and you're next. I step forward.

"That's... so *hot!*"

I stop in my tracks as I recognize genuine excitement in her eyes. Shock turns to zeal and a huge smile spreads across her face.

"That's *so fucking hot!* Oh my God, I'm covered with Kevin's blood! It's all over me! Ohhh, it's so warm and slimy! He's like, totally fucking dead!"

This is not cool.

"Wait, you're him, right?" she asks me, still on her knees and dripping red. "You're that Marvin Brimlow guy! Th-They executed you! Did...did you fucking come back from the *dead?*"

I nod.

"Oh my God, this is *so cool!*" Sherri wobbles to her feet, slipping in blood, and I swear, she looks like she wants my autograph. "Are you like, here to *kill us all?*"

I nod again, trying to look menacing.

"Far fucking *out!*" Sherri bounces up and down like a giddy child and steps towards me. "So you're gonna kill me? You're gonna take your big, bloody knife and fucking kill me? You gonna cut me up into little bits?" She caresses her breasts, then moves a hand down between her legs and begins to rub.

Jesus, this bitch is *fucking crazy!*

"Do you want to fuck me while you do it?" she continues, walking forward and tracing her fingers across my chest. "Do you want to fuck me hard while you're stabbing me to death? Do you want to do it nice and slow, take your time? Make it hurt? Oh God, Marvin! Please, please do it to me!"

"Jesusth! Whad da' fug isth wong wifth you?"

I back up but she keeps coming on to me. She's trying to touch my chest and talk dirty, and honestly, it's skeeving me out.

"Oh please, Marvin! Touch me! Put your filthy hands all over me... Oh, they're so big! Oh God, choke me to death while you're fucking me, *please!*"

Ew. This chick is gross. I don't even want to touch her now, let alone get all up in there. Man, this is a new one for me! What do I do? This is throwing off my mojo.

"I don't know why, but it gets me so hot!" she keeps babbling. "All I ever do is fantasize about dying! Dying a slow, painful, horrible death! I can't help myself! Please, Marvin! Make me suffer! Fuck me in the ass and skin me alive! Rip my arms out of the sockets! Tear me apart and—"

SHUNKK!

I whip the knife into the psycho-bitch's temple, killing her instantly.

Shut up.

I leave the blade lodged in her skull and let her dead body collapse. She spasms before finally going limp. A puddle of blood begins to spread.

There you go, Mr. Black, I killed a couple people with a big knife.

Whew, that's enough of that. Typically, my victims *don't* like what I do to them.

There's that ratty boombox on the floor, still playing that garbage music. During the joy of bloodshed, I'd completely forgotten about it. My initial instinct is to smash the damn thing, so I raise my foot high... but then I have a change of heart. I can use this little radio as a tool, like bait at the end of a lure. Fishing, my friends, fishing.

So I scoop up the scratched-up, stickered-up shitbox, and turn the power off.

You're coming with me, little guy.

CHAPTER 9

OKAY, I think I'm gonna murder the cripple next.

I don't particularly hate the guy, he's just... kind of a boring guy. But his name's on the list and he's an easy target, so there you go. I remember him and Minnie Mouse heading off towards the ruins of the west dorm, so I circle around outside and go that way. But as I get closer to the west dorm, it's clear they aren't in there. Unless they've turned their flashlights off and are being really quiet.

They don't know I'm here yet, so, doubtful.

The ruins are dark and silent. Even if Matt and Hillary did come here, I doubt they'd stick around long. Not exactly a romantic spot. Nobody wants to get it on in a pile of rubble and ashes. Well, that nutbag Sherri probably would have...

Where would I go if I were them? Probably out back, the basketball courts, the garden. Nice, flat pavement for him to roll around on. Yeah, I'll go check that out. As I walk around the building, I notice that none of my little flying buddies are following me. Guess they're all watching the kids, just waiting for me to pop up. Okay, well let's first see if I'm right.

I peek around the corner and yup, I'm right.

There's two flashlights moving around in the garden. I move in closer to confirm, and yup, it's Minnie Mouse and Biceps On Wheels. Looks like they're strolling around in the moonlight, getting to know each other. He's telling her his sob story about how he got paralyzed, and she's watching his arms flex with every push of his wheels. In the air around them, three of the little drone fuckers. They're ready for action.

I sneak closer. Closer. I reach the edge of the garden, which used to be surrounded by lush bushes, and is now just dead branches and weeds. I can see their faces now and barely make out what they're saying.

"...And so I ran, and I jumped, and I pushed the kid out of the way of that truck," Matt says. "Of course, I wasn't so lucky. Now the doctors say I'll never walk again."

"Oh, my God! Oh, you're so *brave!*" Hillary's eyes are wide, her mouth agape. "I'm so sorry, Matt." She strokes his shoulders tenderly.

"Ah, it's okay. I wasn't worried about myself. Just couldn't let anything happen to that poor little kid, y'know?" He shrugs. "But it's okay. I stay busy, workout, have fun. Next month I'm competing in the Chicago Paralympics. Gonna take the gold, you just watch!"

"I bet you will," she says, then starts to blush. "So, uh... does everything else work okay?"

"Everything...*else?*"

They lock eyes. Moonlight shines down on them. Romantic music swells. She sits down on his lap and they kiss passionately. It's disgusting.

Oh, boy. Nerdy little girl so desperately wants to be a dirty little girl. And y'know what? That's fine. I'll let them have their moment. The last two dumbasses I killed right in the middle of the act, and come to think of it, I nailed that squatter couple the same way. Well, not the *same* way, but at the same time and right in the middle of the deed. So with these two, I'll let them have their moment first.

She's a nice girl, and at the very least deserves one good dickin' before being slaughtered. And him saving that little kid? I'm a cruel, sadistic, cold-hearted bastard, but I do have standards and principles. I'd say that being a good samaritan, saving a kid's life and risking his own, that's got to count for something. So, I'll let Biceps On Wheels bust one last nut before dispatching him. I'll even make it relatively quick and painless. Some people deserve to suffer, others can just be snuffed out.

A minute into their little make-out session, Hillary pulls back. Looks like something is wrong. Her eyes go wide and her face turns green.

"Oh... Oh, my God..." she says, looking woozy.

"You okay?"

"I don't... I don't feel so good... Oh, my God!"

She suddenly jumps off his lap and stumbles over to the dead bushes. Dropping to her knees, Minnie Mouse blows three kegs worth of chunks all over the damn place. Well, it looks like three kegs worth, anyway. Biceps rolls over to be tender and supportive, and after a minute, she gets it all out and stands back up.

"S-Sorry," she says. "I don't usually drink."

"Hey, happens to all of us. You okay?"

"I think I need to clean myself up a bit. There's water bottles in the coolers, right?" she asks. Matt nods. "Wait here for me?"

"I'm not going anywhere," he says with a compassionate smile.

She excuses herself and trots off, presumably to their little base camp, leaving Matt all alone. With me. Now's my chance to try the new trick. I'll turn on the boombox and play some of that Neo-Punk shit, he'll hear it and think it's his friends. Then when he comes around the corner to find them, *whack!* Meat cleaver to the fucking face.

The fans will be happy because it'll be bloody and cool looking, and it'll also be quick and painless. Poor Biceps won't even know what hit him. See, I can be compassionate sometimes. I smile and am about to press the play button, when I notice Mr. Hero looking around. Seems like he's checking to make sure the coast is clear.

Once he determines nobody's around, Matt stands up out of his chair and walks over to the bushes to take a piss... Wait a minute, *what??* Matt is standing up and *walking?* It takes a few seconds for my brain to actually register what I'm seeing, but then it hits me like a wave.

My blood begins to boil.

Oh, you little fuck. Oh, you dirty little *fuck*.

I can't believe it! I feel betrayed! I was gonna take it easy on you, make it nice and quick and painless. But oh boy, this is low. Pretending to be a cripple just so you can get a little scoop of ass? I mean, that's bad, even for me. And I'm a horrible serial killer from Hell. Oh buddy-boy, your ass is *mine* now. I'm gonna make this fucking *hurt*.

As I seethe in anger and watch him from the shadows, Scumbag On Wheels finishes draining his lizard and shakes it off. Time to go fishing. I hit the play button on the boombox, and that nauseating bile comes pissing out of it. Right away, Matt hears it and hurries back to his chair.

"Hello?" he says, sitting back down and looking into the darkness towards the music. "Kevin, Sherri? That you?"

Yes, it's them. Come closer.

Matt pushes himself slowly down the walkway in my direction. He's coming into the shadows. All is quiet. I'm behind a tree, deep in shadow, completely invisible. A little bit closer, and he's mine. No meat cleaver to the face for you, shit-brick. That would be too humane. I don't know how I'm gonna do it yet, but it will be brutal and painful. But first, just a little closer...

"Guys? Is that you?" Matt asks, only a few feet away now.

I tense my body, ready to pounce. Ready to tear him limb from limb. Ready to reach up his asshole and pull his head back out through it. Here we go, buddy... here we go... just about time...

Now! I pounce —

I'M SUDDENLY YANKED BACK through the veil and crash down on the stage floor of the arena. Oh, motherfucker! It's the end of the first period. I have to take a one-minute break whether I like it or not. *Fuck!* Why does this always happen right when I'm about to whack somebody?

The fans in the stadium are screaming their heads off. Lights shine down on me from all angles. Fireworks are going off. Ugh, this is frustrating. And of course, there's Jim and my corner men rushing up to me. Ah, Jim. That smile, that dyed-black hair. That gum. Sigh...

"Hey man!" Jim says. "Great job so far! Man, can you believe that little prick in the wheelchair can *walk*?? Oh, the crowd was screaming *so* loud when they saw that!"

"Mmm," I grumble.

"They love you, Marvin!" my cornerman, Turi says. The grubby little guy hands me a bottle of water and a towel. Fine fine, I'll take a sip of water, wipe myself down a bit with the towel. As much as I complain about getting pulled out of the action, it *is* nice to have a little break and get pampered a bit.

I look around at my adoring fans and give them a wave. Everyone cheers. I see David Black out there, The Snapper and his bitches, Satan. They're all ready for more. I look up at the big clock. Ten seconds left. Jim slaps my arm and gives me a wink.

"Have fun out there, killer!" he says, vigorously chewing his gum. I growl at him.

The buzzer sounds and it's game time again.

I stomp back through the portal, and I'm hungry.

CHAPTER 10

I'M BACK, baby.

Oh, Ma-att? Yoo-hoo? Mr. Hero? Mr. Special Olympics? Where could you be? I'm standing right where I was when I was so rudely interrupted, on the dark path along the side of the building. One thing is noticeably missing, the music. I look around and the boombox is gone. Shit. Biceps must have found it and taken it with him. Well, he couldn't have gotten far.

I move around back. He probably went that way again, expecting his booty call to return soon. And sure enough, I'm right again. Damn, I'm good at this shit. Matt is back in his chair, wheeling around the dingy courtyard between the garden and the basketball courts. He's got a flashlight in one hand, and the boombox on his lap.

"Kevin? Sherri? You out here?" Matt slowly spins around, aiming the wimpy beam of light in all directions. "Hillary? Hello?"

Okay dipshit, it's just you and me now.

I stroll forward, coming out of the shadows. This is my magic moment, and it fills my black heart with a wave of happiness. There's a special kind of bond between victim and killer, unlike any other. Every single one of them is a virgin to the experience, and I get the honor of popping their cherries.

The meat cleaver is in my hand. I step onto the courtyard under the full light of the moon. Matt turns, pointing his beam... The light falls on me.

I just stand and smile, cleaver in my hand.

Matt's whole face drops and his throat makes a cute little sound like he just swallowed a frog. He's in shock, staring up at seven feet of redneck beauty. My gore-soaked overalls. My hairy shoulders. My mangled, scarred face. It takes him a second until the shock wears off, and then he screams like a little bitch.

His ass is out of that chair in a flash as he starts bolting across the basketball courts to escape. Nope, I'm not chasing you, Speedy Gonzalez. Instead, I launch the meat cleaver through the air and I hear it *shhunk* into his lower back.

Biceps yelps as the blade severs his spinal cord and takes him crashing to the ground. He smacks face-first into the concrete, shattering his nose and front teeth, and I can hear the delayed echo of the *crack* bouncing off the surrounding walls. Matt trembles and groans, lying helpless in a growing pool of blood. He coughs up broken fragments of his teeth and begins to cry.

I swagger on over.

Seem to be having some trouble walking, my friend? Oh my, it looks like you've been paralyzed! I chuckle and close in. Biceps sputters and whines and tries to crawl away, but he knows it's no use. I step over him, smiling. I enjoy watching him squirm.

"P-Please... p-p-please..." he begs, looking up at me.

"I hape jocksth."

So I grab him by the back of the neck and proceed to drag him further onto the basketball courts. Even though various coaches throughout my childhood begged me to play sports due to my size, it was never for me. Football, basketball, who cares? You run back and forth with a bunch of other dudes, you throw a ball around? And? I never got it.

However, I *have* always wanted to do a slam dunk.

So I drag Biceps to the closest hoop, a tattered, ratty net hanging under it. I lift him up into the air so I can look him in the eye. All he can do is blubber and sob.

"Oh, please... P-Please, God! No! *Ahhhhh!!*" he begs and bitches.

I turn him so I can see his back, and there's that meat clever, buried up to the hilt in his spine just above the hips. So I grab the handle and yank that fucker out of there. Matt screams like a pussy as the gaping wound begins hemor...hemurge...? It begins bleeding a lot.

"OHHH, GOD NO!! PLEASE!! I'M SORRY!!!"

Since there's already a huge, bleeding gash in his back, I may as well open that shit up more. So I swing the meat cleaver again, and again. With two chops, I've cut him nearly in half. I see the absolute agony and shock in his eyes, and I can't help but feel proud. He sputters and gurgles as I slash through his juicy muscles and viscera, and with one final chop, I sever him completely from the waist down.

Matt's legs collapse to the ground as his blood and gizzards splatter down all over. I see the life rapidly draining out of his eyes, so I only have seconds to put a final cherry on top of this sundae. Now's my chance to do a slam dunk.

Still holding Matt—and his upper body—by the back of the neck, I jump high up in the air. I aim for that old, rusty hoop... *Slam dunk!* I smash his head in, snapping and ripping it off with ease.

I land back on my feet and pump my fists in the air as Matt's head bounces to the ground, followed by his body a few feet away. It's not a clean decapitation like you'd get with a blade. Instead, there's a tattered trail of flesh still attached. Yeah, nice and messy, baby! See ya, Biceps. Hope your little girlfriend didn't hear you screaming.

She's next.

Where's that damn radio? Aha, here we go. I find it and scoop it back up. Let's try this again, going fishing. I hide the boombox in the dead bushes of the garden, wincing as I press the play button. More of that garbage comes blasting out. Now I just have to hide and wait.

So I circle around and duck down behind some dead rose bushes. My little hummingbird-fucker friends hover close by. The fans back in Hell must all be on the edge of their seats. Waiting. Waiting. Finally, I see her coming from across the courtyard.

That little bob of brunette hair. That perky little body. That cute but not-quite-cute-enough face. Little girl next door, trying to expand her horizons. Don't worry, Red Riding Hood, I'll make this quick. Unlike your douchebag boyfriend, I believe you're actually a decent person. I mean, you're a ditzy, dumb fuck, you're just another lamb chop to me, and you're gonna die, but you don't deserve to be *tortured.*

"Matt?" she calls out, timidly looking around.

Hillary follows the sounds emanating from the boombox. It sounds to me like some angsty teenager just screaming while his buddies—who can't play instruments—pound away on the drums, bass, and guitar as loud and fast as possible. She comes closer down the path, the light in her hand trembling.

"Matt, where are you? I heard a scream."

She continues walking, getting close now.

She stops in front of the stairs leading down into the garbage bay and loading dock, shining her light inside and calling out for Biceps again. Her back is to me and she's close. This is my chance. I come out from my hiding spot and sneak up on her.

Think I'll do just a simple head crush. The fans love it, as it's incredibly graphic and goopy and cool, but it's also pretty quick and comparably humane. I'll just come up behind her, wrap my hand around her head, and *pop,* squash it like a grape. She'll never know what hit her.

I reach out. Almost there.

"Matt? Come on, quit playing around!"

One more step and I'll be in range to squeeze. But suddenly, she decides to turn around. And there I am about to wrap my huge, gnarly hand around her head, so yeah, she flips the fuck out. Hillary screams and flails her arms as I reach for her. She jerks back and suddenly finds no ground under her feet.

She tumbles down the long, concrete staircase.

Crack! Crunch! Thomp! Smash!

I stand at the top of the stairs, watching dumfounded as Minnie Mouse topples into the loading bay. She screams and gasps and grunts as her bones break and her skin tears. She finally collides with the pavement on the next level, and her blood is already forming into a little red lagoon.

Hillary gurgles and twitches, unable to move. Looks like her back has been twisted and broken into an inhuman angle, with shattered ribs puncturing her lungs. Arms and legs both broken in multiple places, compound fractures jutting the bones through the flesh... Ah man, it's getting me hard. So I grab the boombox—still playing that crap—and stroll down the steps for a closer look.

Oh snap, the left half her face was ripped off at the point of impact. Her tongue is swelling out of her mouth and choking her. She's quivering, suffering, going into shock. Well, shit. So much for making this quick for you, sweetie. Sorry.

Way to go, Marvin.

I can't tell if she knows I'm here or not, as she's basically just a quivering puddle of goo at this point. But I think it's time I end this for her, and I think for this one, I'll kill two birds with one stone. So I raise the boombox over my head and turn the volume all the way up, blasting that shit. With one stout strike, I smash it down.

Brains. Sparks. Blood.

All in a day's work.

CHAPTER 11

LET'S GET SOMETHING STRAIGHT, I am lazy by nature and do not like to work. Do I love to kill? Of course. But there's a difference between doing something for fun and doing it as your job. Back in my previous life, and before I was arrested, it wasn't like I killed someone every day or anything. Not even every week sometimes, but just when I felt like it. And when I did, it was usually just one person; only a couple times in my life had I killed more than one person at the same time.

But now? Now I have to go and slaughter a dozen people in one night, and take my time with it, *and* make it creative and exciting for the crowds. Ugh. It's tiring. It's a *job*. And I've just about had enough of this day at work. I know there's another period break coming up soon, but it's not like I *have* to make this last the full time. I've drawn this out a good bit already, given them a good show, right?

So here's the plan. I'm gonna take care of the remaining members of the Lollypop Guild relatively quickly. No more hiding in the shadows for hours and sneaking around. Time to amp up this tempo. I just want to go home, get out of these clothes, take a shower, and jerk off. Okay?

I'll probably find the others back inside, so off I go, enjoying the serenity of the night. Cool concrete and dead leaves under my feet. The moon shining down. A gentle breeze. Some moron's guts dripping down my back and drying in my ass crack...

I step through the side entrance to the main building and head inside. The two knives are gone, and I left the cast-iron skillet back near the front doors. Shit. Okay, gotta find a weapon. Well, I don't *have* to, but I want to. So as I search for the others, I'm also keeping an eye open for any items that could be used to implement extreme pain and death. So far nothing.

Moving through the main building, I close in on their base camp. Nothing. Everything is silent and dark, except for the candles they left lit. They better not have gotten away on foot. Shit. I am not *running* after anyone tonight.

Getting nervous, I hurry up the stairs and start looking around the second floor. I begin the painstaking process of creeping down every hall, peeking into every room. I have one flying drone fucker following, passing through the walls like a ghost. It's making me a little self conscious, actually. What if these snot-nosed little fuckers just hot-footed it up the road and called the police? Shit.

Fuck that, I am undeterred. I'm gonna find them, damn it.

Up to the third floor, and here things are starting to get a little charred. Some walls are completely burned down, while others are untouched. Still, what an absolute mess. Each office is just filthy, with old papers and pens and furniture strewn around. I move through them all just to be thorough, in case one of my little piggies is hiding in here. There's the accounting office, there's human resources, psychiatrist's offices, admin offices, bathrooms, break room, and file storage.

It takes a while and I don't find any fresh meat. The next floor up is just a burnt cinder, so I sorely doubt anyone's up there. I stroll into the file storage room, a large, dark space filled with file cabinets. A few have fallen over, some drawers are open, and lots of files are covered in dust on the floor. I see one cabinet marked 'B.'

Hmmm, I wonder.

The rusty drawer squeaks as I pull it open. I look down at the folders inside—yup, it's patient files. No way my file is still in here, right? Fuck it, I start flipping through the folders in alphabetical order. I can barely see the labels in the dark, but there it is, way in the back: Brumlow, Marvin R. Sigh... do I dare? Fuck it.

I pull out my folder and open it up. It's too dark to read in here, so I head for the door and start back down the stairs. Gotta get me some moonlight, or a flashlight, candle, something. I get back to the main entrance and it's a little better; the candles are still burning in base camp, moonlight shining through the windows.

Okay then. Let's see what this thing says.

Right on the first page is my police mugshot and my hospital patient-intake paperwork and photo. Hey, good lookin'. This is followed by charts and doctor notes. There is a basic medical/psychiatric work-up sheet, with everything from my height and weight to family medical history, allergies, previous surgeries, etc.

Boriiiiiing.

This is followed by a short section of photos, starting with newspaper clippings, and then a few stills of me and my family before... the incident. I sigh. There I am. There's my whole face. My nose, my lips, my nice square jaw. All before I stuffed a revolver under my chin and blew the bottom half of my idiot face off.

There's me with my wife, Clara, and my two little ones, Billy and Sophie. Everyone is smiling. This photo was taken just a few months before I... sigh. Stupid, stupid, stupid. Damn it, Marvin, why'd you have to go and do that? You could have just left, hit the road. You didn't have to... poor kids. Man, I'm such a bastard. Evil fucking bastard.

Let's see... *"Patient denies past history of psychiatric illness or treatment,"* blah blah blah, *"Patient is not taking psychiatric medications. Current conditions include DM adult onset, hypertension, bilateral lumbar radiculopathy, back pain, bilateral knee pain, BPPV,"* blah blah blah, *"medical management includes aspirin, 500 mg, diphen-hydramine hydrochloride, 25 mg, Lisinopril-HCTZ 20..."* Jesus, who thinks of these fucking names?

"Mr. Brumlow has lived alone in Chicago most of his life. He admits to enjoying isolation. He states that he wasn't popular among his peers growing up and was a victim of bullying the majority of his life." Yeah yeah, big surprise there.

"Patient states that his passion for murder includes the feeling of power over his victims. He states that others' fear

is his motivation, and he feels no remorse for any violent actions taken." Well, almost no remorse... *"Previous CT neuroimaging shows damaged frontal lobe and mild cerebral atrophy in patient."* Hm. Whatever that means.

Ah, here we go. *"Diagnosis: 1. Major Depressive Disorder - Reported feelings of emptiness. 2. Generalized Anxiety Disorder - Reported feelings of being on edge or of impending doom. 3. Narcissistic Personality Disorder - Patient has an inflated sense of self-importance and status."* Oh fuck you, Stockton.

"4. PTSD - Linked to violent past and family history. 5. Obsessive Compulsive Disorder - Compulsivity and an urge to have an over-exerted amount of control over situations." Well, yeah. *"6. Antisocial Personality Disorder - Patient reports no friends or family and feeling isolation. 7. Schizoaffective Disorder - This may explain all of his symptomology as a whole, patient has shown major signs of all symptoms listed above."*

It doesn't even mention my good looks or dashing wit!

"Treatment plan: Six months of mental rehabilitation. Weekly visits until further notice. Labs: None. Physical violence threatened. GAF: 8." Whatever that means.

Yup, most of that makes sense. No, I can't control my rage. Yes, I do enjoy the act of killing and making others suffer. Yes, it did probably stem from a childhood full of abuse. But honestly, even without my father's beatings and my mother's neglect, I still probably would have turned out this way. It's just how I was born, it's in my blood.

Towards the back of the folder, one of the notes is an appointment to meet with a Dr. Thompson Wells on

Monday, February 16, 1975. That name sounds familiar. Isn't that the douche that was talking shit about me on TV? What the fuck was he doing meeting with Stockton? Who is this fucking guy?

Well, no time to think about it now, because out of the blue I hear a scream. It's distant and muffled, but I know my screams. This isn't an *"Ow, I hit my funny-bone!"* scream or an *"Eek! I saw a rat!"* scream. This is specifically a *"Holy fucking shit, I've just stumbled upon a dead, dismembered human body"* scream.

The east building. Somebody's found my handiwork. I smile and drop the folder for now, stomping off down the hallway. Time to go fishing.

CHAPTER 12

BACK OUTSIDE. This here's the little courtyard between buildings. A nice place for staff to have lunch and smoke cigarettes. I walk down the pathway to the east building, trying to keep my big head as low as possible. Before I can play, I need to determine who screamed, where they are, and if they're alone or not. So for now, I'm doing my ninja thing.

I peek my head into the side door of the east building, looking around. All quiet. But wait, no. I do hear something, sounds like people talking. Pretty muffled though, probably coming from outside. Crap, I'd better hurry. So I plod through the building, following the sound, and realize they're in the front parking lot.

When I reach the broken front windows, I can see all three of them. Natasha, Johnny, and Crystal. Looks like Johnny and Natasha are trying to calm down a very distraught Crystal. Hee hee. She's ranting and raving while the other two hold onto her arms, keeping her from falling over.

"Crystal, please slow down," Johnny says.

"Y-You guys... I c-can't... D-Dead! Th-They're dead..." Crystal raves.

See, this is the kind of emotional impact I hope to achieve with my work.

"Who's dead, Crystal?" Natasha asks.

"K-Kevin and Sh-Sherri! D-Dead! ...B-Blood... Oh my God..."

I watch as the handsome young couple—are they a couple? I still don't know—tries to get information from the poor thing. They're asking where Matt and Hillary are. They're asking Crystal to show them where Kevin and Sherri are. She's saying hell no, like any normal person would.

"No! No, we've got to get out of here!" Crystal cries, pulling away from them and running for the main building.

"Crystal!" Natasha shouts.

"Come on," Johnny says. "We have to check it out. See if it's true about Kevin and Sherri."

"What about Hillary and Matt?"

"We have to find them too."

"Look, this is a bad idea. Why don't we just go get some help?"

"We can't just leave them behind!"

They squabble, but ultimately it's Strong Leading Man pulling Miss Knowitall along to investigate the east dorms, off to save the day. Yes, go. Give me some time alone with Crystal. Mmmmm. It's times like this that I really love my job.

I go back to the main building.

There's still candlelight flickering inside through the windows, and I hear the sounds of distress and commotion. As I get closer and look in, I can see

Crystal running around, panicked, gathering up her belongings. Probably also looking for a set of car keys. Sorry honey, that ain't gonna help you. Big Marvin's about to say hello and have some fun. Ever see a dog with a play-toy?

Okay, I really want to surprise her and make a good entrance on this one. I think I'm gonna step behind the veil again, then come out right behind her and get a great big scream. So I head on in and do just that. Once behind the veil, in that cold and misty place once again, I enter the building and find that shitty little base camp.

There she is, little Miss Crystal Ball. She's hysterically throwing her crystals back into her backpack, and yes, it does appear she's also looking for keys. Nope, no keys. Oh, so frustrating, sweetie. What are you gonna do? But she's not alone.

Nope, because right in there with her, but behind the veil, are Hank and Neiman and some of the other fellas. They're all enjoying Crystal's little performance. Especially Neiman. Yup, he's still jerking it.

"Hey, Marvin," Hank says.

"Hey, guysth."

"You here to snuff this little pretty thing out?" Hank asks.

I nod. They all let out jealous moans and groans.

"Oh man, what I would do for some of that," Neiman says.

"You're so lucky, Marvin," says another.

I feel bad for these guys. They're all just trapped in this ashtray for all eternity, and here I am getting to have all the fun. Some guys have all the luck, I guess. I'm about to step through the veil and reveal myself, when I see Crystal do something cute. She has a brilliant idea.

She goes over to her Ouija board.

Ha ha, yes! I clap my hands and laugh as I see her hold the pointer and close her eyes. She's trying to make contact with the other side again. Maybe to ask for help? Maybe to ask where the car keys are? I don't know. But this dummy seems to think it's a bright idea.

"I-I'm calling out to the other side once again..." she chants. "Please, we need help. Is anyone there? Can anyone hear me?"

"Ohhh, I can hear ya, honey," Neiman says, feverishly masturbating.

"Are there any spirits here with me right now?"

Me and the boys chuckle. Yup, *right* here with you.

"P-Please, if you can hear me, try to move the pointer. Just move the pointer to 'yes,' okay?"

"Ah man, if only," Hank says.

They can't move the pointer, but shit, maybe I can. I mean, *I'm* not trapped in purgatory, so let's see. I step right in front of her and reach down, pointing with my index finger. I try to push the pointer, and it actually works! I'm behind the veil and yet, I can still push the stupid pointer thing! So naturally, I push it to "yes."

Crystal nearly recoils, gasping in shock. The boys are impressed too.

"Oh my God! Okay," Hippie-Dippy continues. "Um, me and my friends are in trouble! I think somebody's after us!"

I push the pointer to "yes."

"Can you help?"

I push the pointer to "no."

"W-Well... I'm very scared. What should I do?"

I push the pointer down to the alphabet printed below. One letter at a time, I spell out *"D - I - E."*

Shock and horror comes over her pretty little face. Yes! She begins to back up, trembling, real terror sinking in. Time to make my move; one more second and she's gonna bolt. I'll step through the veil, grab her, and start tearing her apart. Maybe grab that stupid Ouija pointer and bury it in her skull as a nice cherry on top. But then I think about my ghostly companions, here in this world between worlds. Poor Hank and the others, who never get to have any fun...

Y'know what, little girl? You want to make contact with the dead? Allow me to assist.

I suddenly split open the veil right in front of her and lean out. Her eyes snap open wide in fright, and she starts to scream, but my hand is around her throat in an instant. And then, instead of me coming out, I yank her back *in*.

Hank and the fellas shout in delight as I pull Crystal into the world between worlds. Purgatory. Poor little thing chokes and gasps and kicks at me feebly, and as much as I'd like to do so many horrible things to this little dumpling, this one isn't for me. So I drop her to the floor.

Crystal lands into a heap, coughing and holding her throat.

"She'sth aww yaw'sth, guysth," I smile and nod.

Crystal suddenly realizes that we're not alone. Standing around her are several men. Burned men, charred men, dead men. They begin to close in on her, their eyes hungry, their mouths dripping. And there it is, that look on her face. I know that look. It's the "oh shit" look. The look of doom that a person gets when they know they're about to die, but not just die... die a horrible, painful death.

"Aw, gee Marvin! You're a real pal!" Hank says.

"Thanks, Marvin!" all the guys agree and join in with gratitude.

Crystal pulls back, but there's nowhere to go. Burned, roasted, blackened hands reach out to grab her. Neiman's pants are around his ankles and his char-broiled prick is in his hand at full mast. He twitches and shakes, his eyes and warped smile bugging out of his head.

"Ohhh, little girl..." Neiman drools. "Sweet, sweet little girl..."

"No..." Crystal whimpers, but she knows this is it. She's done. She's about to be raped and killed by a bunch of burnt, undead criminals for all of Hell to watch. The hummingbird cameras surround us, getting it from all angles. "No!" she finally screams at the top of her lungs. "*NOOOOOO!!!*"

And then they all just pile in on top of her and I don't need to see the rest. I can imagine. Besides, I've got two more little piggies I need to take care of...

CHAPTER 13

LOGIC DICTATES that once Natasha and Johnny discover the bodies in the east dorm, or any of the others, that they're gonna flip their shit and run. And the only place I know for sure they're gonna run is back to their car. So instead of wandering around and trying to find them in here, I'll just wait by the car. See, lazy by nature.

Fishing.

So I walk to the main entrance and stroll back out into the pleasant night air. The shitty pickup is right there in the big driveway where I left it. Somewhere inside, I hear the muffled sounds of screaming. Ah yes, they're finding the juicy stuff. Wish I could see their faces right now, hear what they're saying.

Oh well, I can always watch the tape tomorrow at home. My hummingbird friends are capturing everything that I can't see, so I'm sure there's at least a couple flying around them, showing what they're doing.

Any minute, they'll come running through the front door, or from around one of the sides of the building, panicked, terrified. And if they discover the pickup has been disabled, they'll just bolt down the long driveway, back out onto the main road. Obviously I can't let that happen, so I stroll across the gravel driveway to block their escape path. Once I pass the pickup, I go out a bit further, then duck off the road into the trees and bushes.

I have a good, clear view of the truck and the building, so now I just wait... And wait. I lean against a tree, tapping my foot. Anytime now, people. Sigh... this sucks. They couldn't have escaped through the back woods, or maybe —

I hear a scream. Aha, yes! Sounds like it's coming from outside, from around back. Then another! Ooooh, they must have just found Matt and Hillary! Hee-heeee, I'm bouncing up and down like a giddy little boy about to meet Lynda Carter. Any minute now, they'll come running out. Any minute...

Boom. There they are.

Johnny comes sprinting around the west building, pulling Natasha behind him by the hand. In his free hand, his trusty Louisville Slugger. In her free hand, a flashlight. The look in their eyes is pure horror as they scramble and trip across the gravel, racing to get to the shitty Toyota pickup.

"Crystal!" Natasha screams. "*Crystal!!*"

"She's dead! They're all dead! *Come on!*"

"You don't know that! We can't just leave her!"

"*I said come on!!*"

They make it to the pickup and, oh look, Stud Muffin found himself the keys. Probably pulled them out of Kevin's blood-soaked pocket. I smile as they jump inside and lock the doors. This should be good.

Johnny turns the key, but of course the engine won't start. He tries again, again, again. The motor clicks and sputters, but won't turn over. He pounds on the wheel and curses in frustration. Yessss. I remain in the shadows and watch as my two young friends desperately squabble and try to figure out what to do. Finally, they decide —

"We have to make a run for it," Johnny says.

Okay, here we go. Just about my moment. Ready, set...

Johnny and Natasha bolt out of the cab, grab hands, and continue running. There's only one road out of here, and they are counting on it to save them... Nope. Not happening.

Instead, I step out from behind my hiding place and stroll into the center of the road, coming into the light. And there I am, seven feet tall, four hundred pounds, caked in blood and filth. Lightning bolt behind me? No? Damn it, one of these days. It's still dramatic enough.

I smile as they skid to a halt in the gravel, looking up at me and screaming in terror. Man, she's got a great scream, I love it! And by the look in her eyes, I can see that Little Miss Psyche Major recognizes me.

"No, it can't be," she gasps. "It can't be..."

"Come on!!"

Johnny yanks her back the way they came, frantically scrambling back towards the building. I follow them nice and slow, taking my sweet fucking time. They make it to the main entrance, pushing the doors closed behind them on rusty hinges. As I approach, I hear the sounds of smashing and heavy objects being moved around. Ah yes, they're trying to barricade the door. How cute.

I make it to the doors and can still hear them inside, hurrying around, arguing, doing who cares what. A quick push on the door and I can tell there's something pushed against it. Maybe a table or a couch? There wasn't exactly a whole lot of furniture left in there, if I recall. Either way, it won't be a problem. I could just push it in easily with one blow, but I want to ratchet up the fear a bit.

So I bang and shake on the door. I shove it in a little, then a little more. I don't hear my little piggies anymore, so I have to assume they've run off and are hiding. Well, I don't want them getting too far, so with one final kick, the door blasts open, and I'm in. All is dark and quiet inside.

A few candles remain burning in the base camp area. No signs of anyone around. I creep inside slowly, surveying the area. I know that on the other side of the veil, Hank and Neiman and the boys are having an undead, bar-be-cue gangbang with little Crystal in this very room, but I'll leave them be. I've got two more to deal with and I can't let them get away.

Johnny and Natasha must have run deeper into the building. I don't see anything in here that could be useful. Before I continue on, I remember to pick up the file folder with all my patient history inside, but wait... Where is it? I left it right there on the floor, didn't I? I look around, thinking it might have been pushed off to the side somewhere during the commotion, but nothing.

Wait a minute. Did that cunt *take* my fucking file?

Before I can even start brewing with anger, I hear something from up on the second floor. They're up there, all right. So I charge over to that big ol' staircase and I stomp my way up. I reach the top of the stairs and land in my best football pose, ready to pounce. But unfortunately, I'm not the one who pounces.

KRAKK!!

I don't really see the baseball bat coming, only a quick blur, followed by explosive pain between my eyes. If I still had a nose, the blow would've shattered it. Even so, I have fireworks going off in my head and my equilibrium is all fucked. I rock back on my heels, teetering on the edge of the stairs. Little fucking Johnny Quest looks pretty happy with himself, finally getting to play the hero.

"Natasha, run!" he shouts and hits me again, this time in the stomach.

I double over, the wind knocked out of me, and catch a glimpse of Miss Blondie come out from her hiding place. And she's holding my folder. She tries to run past me, but I lash out and she squeaks, jumping back. As I flail madly, trying to catch my balance, I reach out and grab the railing on top of the bannister. A large section of it rips off, breaking the frame in half and exposing a row of jagged stokes still sticking up.

"Run!" Johnny says again, continuing to beat on me with his bat.

But I'm sprawled across the top of the stairs, trying hard not to topple down them, and I don't think she's dumb enough to try getting past me. Still, that damn Louisville Slugger keeps coming down, and I've had enough. This shit hurts. The next time this dumb fuck swings, I reach up and catch the bat.

With a hard yank, I rip it out of his hands and send it flying away. Natasha screams as I stand back up, my own blood trickling down my face, murder in my eyes. Oh, buddy boy, you are gonna *get it.*

"Run, Natasha! *Run!*"

"Johnny, come on!"

"Just run!" he shouts, pulling a butterfly knife from his pocket.

Aha, he must've taken it off Kevin when he discovered his corpse. Now he's flipping it open and waving it at me as I get to my feet, his hands trembling. He lashes it at me again and again, so I reach out to grab his wrist.

But this fucker is fast, and before I know it, he's ducked and pivoted away, swinging the knife at my hand. And he actually gets me, the little bastard. Slices open my palm right in the meat of the thumb, and it fucking hurts! I pull my hand back, grunting in pain, and before I know it, he lunges forward again.

Johnny fucking Quest stabs me right in the gut.

He gasps and stumbles back, shocked at the sight of what he's done. I look down in shock myself. The blade is stuck in my belly right up to the fucking hilt. Motherfucker! Thankfully, I'm a big, sloppy pig, so it's just lodged in my fat, not even scratching any vital organs. I pull the knife out and snarl as hot blood begins running from the wound. I step forward.

"Natasha, run!"

Johnny staggers backwards as I begin to corner him. He uses his jive, fancy footwork to try and fake me out, get past me, but nope. With my arms spread wide, there's no way he can get around. Still, he tries, faking left and then bolting right, trying to get around me.

Not happening.

I catch him by the arm like a child and fling him through the air. And shit, I wasn't planning this or even aiming for it, but Blondie Boy just so happens to land right on the fragmented section of the spokes in the bannister. Four of those broken spokes pierce through his body, ripping up through the chest cavity. Damn, couldn't have planned it any better!

"*NOOOOO, JOHNNY!!!*"

Ah, I love hearing a woman scream.

Johnny boy spits up blood, gagging, trembling, all that good stuff I like. One of the spokes is poking up through his lung, another just missing his heart, and the other two are down in his gut. The sight of this yuppie douche bag choking on his own blood, his feathered hair ruffled, his nice clothes ruined... this is why I do what I do.

I approach to admire my handiwork, watching little Johnny squirm and struggle helplessly. He looks up at me, tears in his eyes. Here you go, mister actor. You finally get to do your big death scene.

I take the blood-streaked butterfly knife that he stabbed me with, and I return the favor. This time, I plunge the point straight down into his bitch mouth. He spasms and sputters and bleeds, and the horror in his eyes finally fades away. He's gone.

End scene.

"*NOOOO!!! NOOOO!!! AAAIIIEEEEE!!!*"

Natasha weeps and wails, nearly collapsing in shock. Sorry about your boyfriend, sweetie. Were they even an item? I still don't know... In any case, she's backing up, and still clutching my file. She bumps into the next stair-case heading up and falls on her ass. Only one way to go now, sweet cheeks. Up.

And she does indeed go up, screaming and wailing

for help. Nobody's gonna help you now, toots. I yank the knife out of Johnny's dead skull and lumber after her, gripping the bleeding wound in my belly. The slash in my hand hurts like fuck, too. But up we go, into the burned top half of the building.

This should be interesting.

CHAPTER 14

I REACH the top of the stairs on the third floor and take a second to catch my breath. Too many stairs. I'm tired. I look both ways down the long hall and think I hear movement to the left. So I head in that direction, through the dark, partially-singed corridor. Little Miss Women's Lib must be hiding out in one of the offices or storage areas. The old carpet is now caked in layers of condensed ash. Cobwebs everywhere, a rat runs across the floor... Jesus, any second now, Count Dracula's gonna pop out!

I go door to door, but don't see shit. Maybe I was wrong, maybe she's at the other end of the hall. Okie dokie, off I go. I stalk down that way, left hand clamped against the gut wound, blood oozing between my fingers. And once again, door to door, taking my time. Nice and slow.

And shit, I don't see or hear anything down at this end of the hall either. This bitch plays a mean game of hide and seek! But I'm not deterred. I check the bathrooms, the broom closest, storage room... nothing. I check the offices and employee break room, still noth—Wait a minute.

Here on the table in the break room is my Psych file.

The folder is open, and the papers inside obviously have been spread out and rummaged through. Has this ditz actually been reading up on me? Pain in the ass. I shake my head and put the knife down for a second, scooping the papers back into a neat pile, then close the folder back up. The whole thing gets folded in half and stuffed deep into my big pants pocket. Not losing that again. Gonna make for good toilet reading.

I come back out into the hallway, and all eight of my little flying friends are hovering around. Hm, that's weird. Usually all of them aren't in the same place together unless me and the victim are both... oh, shit.

WHACKK!!

Old broomstick right to the balls. Bitch was hiding in the hall behind a pile of rubble, just waiting for me. I double over in pain, dropping the knife. She screams and wastes no time bolting away, the broomstick falling from her grip. I dive in front of her, keeping her from heading back down the main hall, and she squeaks, running the other way.

I scoop up the bloody knife and follow.

She's going for the side stairs. Gonna run down, get outside, head for the road... Fuck! I pick up the pace, my bleeding gut screaming at me, my lungs begging me to rest. I smash through the door to the side stairwell and am about to start bounding down the stairs when I notice something peculiar.

Natasha isn't running downstairs. She's going up.

Oh, come *on*. So I keep chugging, climbing up that next flight of stairs to the fourth floor, and here the serious fire damage really becomes apparent. But wait...

She's not stopping at the fourth floor, she's going up to five! What the hell? Even walking around on the fourth floor is dangerous, it's nearly completely burned. But the fifth floor? Shit, I didn't even bother going up there when I first got here.

Nothing up there but the blackened skeleton of the building. Probably can't even walk up there without breaking through what's left of the floors. But if that's where you're going, little darling, that's where I'll follow. Hm, that could be a love song... Anyway, I follow.

The stairs at the top nearly break beneath my weight, and as I step through the stairwell door, I enter a charred wasteland with no ceilings and barely any floor. The moonlight shines down on the burnt ruins, the breeze up here stiff and chilly. Everything is charred, completely destroyed. I feel like if I even touch some of these support beams, they'll just crumble.

So I take it nice and easy. Slow, careful steps. The blackened boards creak under my feet, warning me that I'd better fuck off, or else. But I keep going, stepping only on the spots less likely for me to break through. There's not many of those spots, though; nearly half of the floor has fallen through, with only a few weak floor boards remaining. A fragile piece of lattice work. Ugh.

Two crows suddenly shoot out from behind some rubble and startle the horseshit out of me. But I hold it in. The cameras are here, people are watching. I get my shit together and begin creeping forward again, when suddenly —

Out she pops, little Miss Psyche Major coming out from behind the same pile of rubble as those crows, running like hell. She books it right past me, and I instinctively reach for her and give chase. I don't even seem to realize or care that she's running across the real shitty part of the floor. She's a sweet little pixie, able to easily jump across the few strong support beams. I'm not.

At the very moment that I realize this little bitch has tricked me, the floor gives way and I crash through. Suddenly, my feet are dangling in the air and I'm clinging to the charred structure, in a hole up to my chest. I kick and thrash and try to pull myself up, but I can feel the integrity of these support beams rapidly crumbling.

Oh, fuck.

Little Miss Thang has made it to a safe spot and watches me from a distance, catching her breath. Bitch! I try to scramble, but it's no use. Satisfied that she's bested me, Natasha turns and runs off to the nearest staircase. In a second, she's gone, heading downstairs, running for the door... Fuck!

The boards groan and crack, and I know what's coming next.

It's inevitable, like a roller coaster climbing up to that first peak, you know it's gonna drop. And drop, I do. Finally, it all just collapses in on me, and I'm falling. Soot and ashes and fragments of wood in my face. I smash through the fourth floor and finally stop on the third.

I collide onto the floor along with a shitload of filth and debris, and my ears are ringing. My head is throbbing. My gut is burning. My hand is stinging. My back is aching. I'm all covered in soot and ash and dried blood, and I can't do nothing but lay here for a minute and catch my breath.

There's a huge hole I've made in the ceiling above. One of the hummingbird fuckers flies through the wall and finds me, focussing its lens for all the fans to see me in this state. Damn it, no privacy. Guess I'd better move, can't let them see me down. Ugh. This feminist bitch is gonna fucking *pay*.

I pull myself up and dust off a bit, hurting all over. I look around for the butterfly knife but it's lost and I'm not about to go digging in rubble for it. So, off I go again, stumbling forward, pissed. It takes a minute to even figure out where I am in all this darkness and mess, but I manage to find my way back to the main staircase. Then I hear a noise.

The cafeteria.

That's right, the stairs she ran down would lead her there, so off I go in that direction. I hurry, limping, out of breath, holding my bleeding stomach wound. Finding my way through the dingy maze, I make it to the back end of the slop hall. There's a dividing wall of frosted windows, many now broken, and guess who I see on the other side!

There she is, Natasha, obviously thinking she's finished me. She trudges through the rows of tables, crying and sniffling, still hurrying, but not running. No sense of urgency.

I see her moving along the wall of windows, making her way for the exit, trying to get out to the main road and find some help. Perfect timing. I move up to the windows, waiting for her. Almost, almost...

SMASHHH!!!

I punch through that fucking window and send shards of glass flying in at her. Natasha lets out a scream with a really nice vibrato, jumping into the air, her hands flailing wildly. I reach for her, leaning halfway through the window frame, but she's already stumbling back and running. No time to lose, I launch myself forward, crashing through glass and wood and sheetrock and landing in the cafeteria.

Natasha is now bleeding from multiple lacerations, little shards of glass sticking out of her pink skin. Her eyes bulge with terror as she looks back and sees me following. Yelping like a little squirrel, she scrambles forward through the next available doorway, the kitchen. I hear her bolt the door from the inside, and I smile.

Like that shit's gonna stop me.

I smash my shoulder into the door and it shakes on its hinges. Hm, stainless steel door, pretty strong. So I pound again, and again. The door is denting and the frame beginning to crack and splinter, but it's still standing. Enough of this shit, precious seconds are ticking away. So I step back, lift my knee up high, and shoot the hardest front-kick I can muster into that door.

That does the trick. The steel crumples and the wooden frame and chunks of sheetrock go flying inward. The sound is like thunder echoing inside a tin can. I hear another squeak of terror from inside, and I know Miss Thang is now cornered. Nowhere to go.

I step through the huge hole I've made into a swirling cloud of dust. And there she is, across the dark room, her back against the wall. No time to look for another door, no time to hide. She trembles and fights back tears as I approach. I could probably find any number of cooking utensils to use as a murder weapon in here, but I think I want to use my bare hands for this one.

My flying friends circle around us, ready for the kill.

"Marvin!" she suddenly cries out.

I stop in place. This should be good.

"M-Marvin... I can't even imagine what it must have been like for you," she continues. "Growing up in an abusive home, being picked on at school... So much trauma. So much sadness. And on top of all that, nobody really *understands*, do they, Marvin? Nobody can ever understand what it's like, can they? You've been so alone, all this time..."

Okay, yeah. That's true.

"Nobody ever asks how *you're* doing, do they? No, they only ever care about themselves. They don't give a shit about anyone who's different. Nah, they'd rather just lock us up in a box and throw away the key."

Us? She steps forward, a look of compassion in her eyes.

"They don't understand greatness when they see it," she says. "They call it a sickness, but what do they really know about the human brain? *They're* the ones who are sick! They don't understand your potential. This world never even bothered teaching you love, only hate!" She steps forward again.

"Your mother only ever taught you that women would let you down, and never love you. Your father only ever taught you violence and cruelty. Oh, I'm so sorry, Marvin!"

Well, I mean, she's not *wrong*.

"So much pain," she goes on, reaching out to tenderly

touch the center of my chest. I wonder if she thinks I don't know she's holding a knife behind her back. "So much suffering. You've never really had anyone you could truly be yourself with, have you? Oh Marvin, I *understand*. I can help. You just have to let me in..."

Fwap! I easily catch her wrist as she tries to jam the knife into my heart.

Her eyes say "oh shit." I smile my twisted grin.

Yes, my father did teach me violence and cruelty. But remember, he also taught me how to fish. And of course, how to gut a fish.

"Sowwy, tsweetie," I say, ripping the blade out of her grip. "I unduhstan'. I ca' hewp. You jus' hab' to wet me in." I aim the point of the knife at her exposed navel and jam that fucker home. She lets me in.

Natasha's eyes flap open wide as she feels the steel cut right through her core and lodge in her spine. She chokes and sputters, looking down at the wound in shock. But we're not done, no no. When you gut a fish, you have to be thorough. You got to saw your way through the fat and muscle in the abdomen—

Shkk! Chufft! Schlop schlop schlop!!

You have to cut through the ribcage, allowing the internal organs to spill out. *Crackk! Shuftt! K-Khak! Schlop schlop schlop!!*

Finally, your fish is splayed wide open.

I toss the knife away and hold little Natasha up by the throat, watching the life fade from her eyes. Her screaming and struggling has stopped. Normally with a fish, you chop the head and tail off, skin it, all that good stuff. But I have something else in mind, something I'd never be able to do without superhuman, evil strength.

I thrust my hand into that open wound, right where I made my first cut at the belly button, and rip through bloody meat until I feel something big and hard. Her spine. Wrapping my fingers around it, I feel the vertebrae crunching as I cinch my grip. Let's see if this works out the way I'm seeing it in my head.

One last quick look at her face and yes, she is still barely alive, in shock, in complete disbelief about what's happening to her. Good, while she's still conscious, I go ahead and put the cherry on top of this kill.

I give her spinal column a good-hard twist, snapping it like a twig, and then I yank it down as hard as I can. Her head is suddenly ripped down through her clavicle and rib cage, shattering bones and tearing flesh. Her bloodied face and hair fold inward like some rubber mask as the skull peels away from the tissue.

Hot blood absolutely gushes everywhere as I give one more hard tug, ripping Natasha's spine and cranium out through the wound in her belly. Little chunks of her face cling to the bloody skull, and her left eye in still in its socket. Her dipshit tongue is hanging out of the mouth, dripping with gore.

Yes! That's exactly how I envisioned it!

"WOOOOO!!!" I howl triumphantly, holding the gooey skull and spine up in the air. The little humming-bird fuckers surround me as I celebrate. I take Natasha's bloody skull and spike it hard like I just made the winning touchdown at the Super Bowl. Yes! I fucking nailed it. I love that I can actually do something like that. Fuck yeah... Hey, I win! I'm done! WOOOOO!!!

I see the veil opening up behind me, calling me back.

My work here is done. So why do I feel like I forgot something...?

Oh, whatever. I can already hear the crowd cheering.

CHAPTER 15

VICTORY!

I step through the veil and back into the Grand Malavista Arena. Ah, home sweet Hell. The crowd roars in applause as I pump my fists into the air. Lights shine in my eyes, and all around me I see the happy faces of my adoring fans. Up on the big screens, slow-motion replays of that last kill are running from multiple angles.

Looking down at myself, I see that all my wounds have now magically healed. This is great. I bow and wave to the crowd, and they love me. Afterlife is good.

An elated Jim runs up to me with my corner team, jumping up and down to congratulate me. David Black and MC Bruno are close behind with a microphone, ready for the post-clash interview. Jim excitedly jumps up and down and starts to hug me, but then thinks better of it.

"Dude! That was great, Marvin! Great kill!" Jim says through a mouthful of bubblegum. "You did it! Almost a perfect score!"

Almost? Huh?

"Marvin! Now that it's all over, how do you feel?"

Bruno asks, holding out the mic for me. "What are your thoughts on the clash?"

"I hab a gweat time," I say. "Now I gotta jus' go home an' tabe a tshowa'."

Everyone chuckles like I'm joking.

"With nearly a 100% kill rate, you must be pleased with your performance!"

"Wha'?" I look over at Jim, then at Mr. Black, confused. "Wha' doesth he bean?"

Jim shrugs. "Just means you got almost all of 'em! You did great!"

Almost all of them? "Oh, no..." My heart drops.

"You know, that little ginger asshole," Jim says, chewing. "Remember, he left earlier in the night for booze, said he was coming right back? Nah, he's long gone."

Ted! Oh no no no...

"Bu' wai'... Wheah isth he?"

"Who knows? Once they leave the kill site, they're gone, out of play," Mr. Black says. "But it's okay. You don't have to get *all* of them. This is still a win! And—"

"Fug!" I snarl and stomp my foot in frustration. Jim and Mr. Black watch me pace around and sulk, confused as to why I'm not happy with these results. "I hab ta go backsth!"

"Marvin, Marvin, the clash is over," Mr. Black says, trying to calm me down.

I look up at the big clock. It's stopped with 6:37 remaining in the period.

"Wook!" I say, pointing to the clock. "I stiww gob dime!"

Jim laughs, looking nervously around at the hungry

crowd of onlookers. "Come on now, buddy. There's less than seven minutes on the clock. We don't even know where the little bastard is. He could be miles away and we wouldn't—"

"Pstaht da cwock again!" I say, turning back to the still-open veil. "I'm goin' backsth in!"

"Marvin, please..."

I shoot him a hard look. You don't become champion by having an *almost* perfect score.

Mr. Black sighs. "Okay, big boy. We'll start the clock back up. But when this period is over, that's it. Game over. Got it?"

I grunt in acknowledgment. The crowd looks shocked that I'm going back. So does Jim. But there is no way, no *fucking way* I'm letting that little carrot-top beanstalk cunt live. Less than seven minutes? I can do it.

The clock starts up again, and I step back through.

HERE I AM, back outside at the main entrance of the Chapman Institute. Back in the cool night air, gravel under my bare feet. Must be the middle of the night. The hummingbird camera fuckers float around me, awaiting my next move. If Ted is still close by, maybe I can hurry and still get the job done. That means *running*. Ugh.

I look down that long, dark driveway, but before I go anywhere, I notice something laying in the gravel. It's that damn cast-iron skillet that I left there earlier in the night. And if I do recall, that baby *was* reserved for Ted. So with a smile, I scoop that bad boy up. Then I take a deep breath... and start running.

Huff huff huff — I'm a big, heavy, sloppy mass of blubber with huge feet, each step smashing into the gravel like a fucking elephant. By the time I'm halfway down the driveway, I'm already out of breath. My lungs are aching. I'm sweating so much, all the dried blood and filth on me is getting juicy again.

By the time I reach the end of the driveway and pass that big wrought-iron gate, I'm staggering forward, holding my side in pain. Sucking huge gulps of air into my lungs, I look around the main road. Still nothing here, but I know the town is only just around the corner. So I keep chugging along. I walk for a few seconds, trying to catch my breath, then start running again. Then go back to walking. This process continues.

I finally reach the end of that dark road, and find some streetlights. There are roads, traffic lights, buildings. I push further ahead, shuffling ahead right into the center of town. It must be three in the morning or something, 'cause the streets are dead. Nobody walking or driving, and no businesses open... except one.

Down the street, I see the neon lights outside Tommy's Tavern, a handful of vehicles still parked out front. As I get closer, one of the cars catches my eye. A shitty, red VW Bug. Ohhh yeah, baby. Ted.

I run forward, really pushing myself. I feel my time rapidly running out. Any second now, the buzzer could go off and I'd be instantly pulled right back. No way. I have to finish the job first. This little schmuck is going down. Nothing fancy, Marvin, just get the job done.

So I open the door of the tavern and step in, ducking my head down to clear the door frame. It's your typical seedy pub. Dark, smoky, dingy. The smell of beer and farts. Pretzels on the counters. Jukebox playing oldies. A tired bartender who looks like she'd rather be anywhere else, and of course, a handful of drunkards getting plastered.

Everybody seems to stop what they're doing and look at the hulking, seven-foot giant covered with dirt and blood who just walked in, out of breath. Mouths hang open. All except one. He sits slouched over the bar, sloppy drunk, a collection of beer bottles gathered around him. I grip the skillet nice and tight, and walk forward.

"Um, hello," the bartender welcomes me warily. "W-Welcome to Tommy's. Is there, um... anything I can do...?"

I walk up behind Ted. He's laughing and talking to himself, though it looks like he thinks everyone in the place is in on the conversation. He finishes off another brewsky and pounds the bottle back down, belching.

"Oh, yeah!" Ted says, slapping the counter. "I think I would like another, please!"

So much for going out to get booze and bringing it back to your friends, eh Ted? Got a little sidetracked, did you? That's okay, you're about to join them anyway.

The bartender backs up in fear as she sees me approaching, coming up right behind Ted, breathing down his neck.

"Um, sir? I-Is this anything I can g-get for..."

Nope. I'm fine. I found what I came for.

Ted suddenly realizes that someone is standing right behind him. He turns around, his eyeballs floating on his face, and looks up at me. I raise the skillet.

SMASH!! CRUNCH!! BASH!!!

Three blows, and Ted's head ruptures and bursts like a fucking melon. The bartender and patrons jump back in terror, screaming.

"Jesus Christ!!"

"Oh my God!!"

I toss the skillet aside and it clanks to the floor. Everyone is in shock, watching the smashed pile of lasagna that used to be Ted's noggin splash all over the bar. Blood and brains and little tufts of red hair splatter everywhere. I calmly watch as the rest of Ted's corpse slides to the floor, and breathe a sigh of relief. The bartender and patrons are frozen, dripping with blood, staring at me.

I look around at them all and nod politely.

There's a cold beer sitting on the bar, so I scoop that baby up and take a swig. Ahh, now that's what I call getting the job done. I turn and stroll out of the bar.

Time to go home. It's been a long day. But rewarding. I wouldn't want to do anything else. Very few people can say that they love their job, but I do. And I'm damn good at it, thank you very much.

Jim is actually right. It's time to renegotiate my contract. I'm ready for the big money.

I'm ready to be the champ.

Jesse D'Angelo is an author and illustrator, born in New York, raised in California, and currently residing in Tennessee with his wife and son. He is a veteran of the film and television industries and has also worked with law enforcement as a sketch artist on multiple criminal investigations.

When not writing books about horrible monsters and brutal serial killers, he spends his time changing diapers, scooping cat litter, and trying to avoid other human beings to the best of his ability.

ALSO BY THE AUTHOR

Lady of the Lake

Skinner

Composite

A Collection of Tails

Prey To God

Doomsday Dogs

Dying Sheep